SOME THINGS...
THE FIZZLEBERT STUMP BOOKS

Wonderfully told, fabulously eccentric, and certain to leave everyone in the family wearing a broad smile.

> – Jeremy Strong

Fantastically funny

> – Primary Teacher

It's a high-wire of daft ideas and deft storytelling, ringmastered by a narrator who intrudes on the action with hilariously incongruous asides. Top fun at the Big Top.

> – Financial Times

One of the funniest books I've ever read!

— Amy, 10, Girl Talk

If you like funny, exciting and entertaining books, read about Fizzlebert Stump. The author keeps the reader gripped by the way he ends each chapter, making you want to read on to find out what happens next. Even my mum enjoyed this book and I had to keep telling her what was happening!

— Freya Hudson, 10, Lovereading4kids

FIZZLEBERT STUMP

AND THE
GIRL WHO LIFTED
QUITE HEAVY
THINGS

A.F.HARROLD

ILLUSTRATED BY
SARAH HORNE

BLOOMSBURY
NEW YORK LONDON NEW DELHI SYDNEY

For Claire, Dom and Freya

Bloomsbury Publishing, London, New Delhi, New York and Sydney

First published in Great Britain in February 2015 by Bloomsbury Publishing Plc
50 Bedford Square, London WC1B 3DP

www.bloomsbury.com

Bloomsbury is a registered trademark of Bloomsbury Publishing Plc

A CIP catalogue record for this book is available from the British Library

ISBN 978 1 4088 5331 3

MIX
Paper from
responsible sources
FSC® C020471
www.fsc.org

Typeset by Newgen Knowledge Works (P) Ltd., Chennai, India
Printed and bound in Great Britain by CPI Group (UK) Ltd, Croydon CR0 4YY

CHAPTER ONE

In which apologies are made and in
which the book begins, more or less

Now, I don't know if you ever watch
the television. Of course I don't, how
could I? This is only the first sentence of the
book and I don't even know your name. We've
not been introduced properly. I'm the chap
telling you this story, my name's probably on
the front cover somewhere (it escapes me
right now), and you are . . . ?

Sorry about that, but that's what happens if you interrupt on the first page. I get distracted. Okay. Here we go. Let's start again.

Ahem.

I don't know if you ever watch the television, but if you do you might have noticed that sometimes programmes have a little sequence before the opening credits. Sometimes it's all the usual characters you see week in and week out (maybe they're sharing a joke or recapping what happened in the last episode), but occasionally it's people you've never seen before. More than that, it's people you don't know doing stuff that makes you wonder if you've even tuned in to the right channel. *What is all this?* you think. But then the theme tune starts and the credits roll and you sit back and forget about it until much

later on when it all becomes relevant. That
is to say: *if you're patient, it'll all make sense in
the end*.

Well, the first chapter of this book is a bit
like that. If you've read one of these books
about Fizzlebert Stump before (the ones I
spent ages writing, so you should read them,
if only out of politeness) you'll notice right
away that he's not in the first scene. In fact,
no one you know is. None of his friends from
the circus where he lives are in it. His mum
(a clown) isn't in it, his dad (a strongman)
isn't in it. Fish (a sea lion) isn't in it. None of
the people you've read about in all the other
books are in it.

And if you've *never* read any of the other
books about Fizzlebert and his adventures
(books that, as I said, I spent ages writing),

then it's probably just as important to let you know that this first chapter's an odd thing, because I don't want you sitting there reading it saying to yourself: 'Well, I don't think much of this writer, he's completely forgotten his main character.' Fizz *will* turn up, if you're patient. Okay? Is that clear? No complaining about this beginning? Thank you.

Now, I'll get on with it.

Scene one.

The first scene.

The beginning of the book. Finally, after all that apologetic preamble. (Preamble is an interesting word actually: *amble* means 'walk around pointlessly', and *pre-* means 'before', so it means: 'a pointless wander round beforehand', which is, if you think about it for a moment and stop interrupting with silly

questions, more or less exactly what just happened.)

As I said: *now we begin*.

It was a dark and stormy night. Lightning flashed like jagged electric spears beneath great black clouds. The rain lashed in roaring gushing sheets from the sky. Windows rattled in their frames, trees rocked this way and that, and the noise of the pouring rain on the roofs of the buildings sounded like a machine gun spraying its bullets across a particularly soggy battlefield.

(That's very descriptive writing, isn't it? Really setting the scene nicely. It was well worth waiting for, don't you think? Sets a high standard for the rest of the book.)

It wasn't the sort of night to be out on. Anyone with any sense was at home, locked in

behind waterproof doors, tucked up under a duvet reading a book by torchlight. Even owls were huddled together in their barns, keeping warm by hooting at each other, except they didn't know they were being hooted at because the storm was roaring too loudly outside to hear a hoot. It wasn't a good night to be an owl.

It wasn't a good night to be a balloonist either. (And by balloonist I don't mean a children's entertainer who folds long sausage-shaped balloons into the dim likenesses of animals or bicycles or historical figures, but the sort of person who flies a hot air balloon.)

You must know what a hot air balloon looks like – a great big upside-down tear-drop thing, full of hot air, with a wicker basket dangling underneath where the

pilot and his or her passengers sit turning the knobs on the burner which shoots out flames, keeping the hot air hot and the balloon in the sky.

Just in case you still don't know what I'm talking about, here comes a balloon now.

Out of the storm a dark shape approaches. A flash of lightning explodes behind it, but all we see is the black silhouette of a hot air balloon and it's getting bigger, it's coming closer.

Now we're inside the balloon's basket. There are two figures looking harassed, panicked, worried and windswept. One is a man and one is a woman and both wear leather flying caps with rain-flecked goggles and have beautiful moustaches that flap about in the storm. Between them is the burner, the thing like a large camping stove that shoots flames into the mouth of the balloon. But tonight the flames are small, and they flicker as if they're about to go out.

'We need more height,' the man shouts, his words barely reaching across the basket before being whipped away on the wind.

'I'm trying. I'm trying,' the woman shouts back, fiddling with the knobs on her side of the burner. 'We need more gas.'

The man rushes to the front of the basket, leans over and looks out into the storm. He lifts his goggles to see better but is forced to squint as the rain lashes his eyeballs.

'A tree,' he shouts suddenly, pointing. 'A tree!'

The basket smashes into the leafy, branchy, bushy head of the tree in question and bursts out the other side.

'More height,' he shouts again, before turning back to the burner to help the woman with one of the controls, which seems to be jammed.

Now, suddenly, the scene changes. The noise quietens. We're indoors. A perfectly

normal farmer is walking across the landing in the early hours of the morning. He's coming from the bathroom where he's just had a wee, going back to his bedroom, where he's been tucked under the duvet with a good book. He pulls the curtain to one side to have a quick look out the window to see if the storm's ending yet. It isn't.

Rain is beating against the glass. Outside he can just about see the dark shapes of trees that separate the farmhouse from the fields, and then . . . Oh! He sees something else.

His jaw drops, his eyes go wide: *something's coming!*

A dark shape in the sky, huge and getting bigger. It's coming straight at him. He sees a flickering spurt of fire in the middle of it and then he thinks he can make out voices, but the

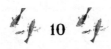

wind is too strong, the rain too loud and the glass in the windows too thick for him to hear what they're saying anyway, and then . . .

CRASH!

A hot air balloon has flown into his farm-house.

And then, if this really were a television programme, just as you were sitting up and paying attention going, 'Oh golly gosh, a hot air balloon has just flown into a house, what a nuisance!', suddenly the credits sequence would start up. That theme tune you know so well would burst into life, all jolly and upbeat, and you'd be tapping your toes, maybe even singing along . . .

Hey! Guys! It's the Fizzlebert Show!
Grab your hat, it's time to go.

Pull on your coat and get in the tent,
an hour with Fizz is an hour well spent.
Thump, thump, thump, thumpity-thump.
This is the show about Fizzlebert Stump!
(or something like that)

. . . and, one after another, each of the characters would appear, turn to the camera and smile as their actor's name is shown underneath, except, of course, in this book there are no actors (except *Alexander Fakespeer, The Man What Does Shakespeare*, an act from another different circus who appears briefly in the background in Chapter Seven).

So, the music's rolling, the song's singing, and a short boy with an enormous beard tumbles across the sawdusty ground, springs to his feet, turns to face the camera and gives

a big thumbs up: *featuring Wystan Barboozul as Wystan Barboozul, The Bearded Boy*.

Then the camera focuses on a huge pair of shoes and slowly pans up, past voluminous silky trousers and a great wobbly silky tummy, until it rests on the sad face of a clown who blinks widely out of the telly before vanishing

behind the surprise arrival (except it happens in the credits every week, so it's no surprise to you) of a custard pie. As the custard drips: *with Mrs Stump as Mrs Stump, The Fumbling Gloriosus.*

A picture of a caravan. A wobbly caravan. The camera pans down to the man underneath the caravan, holding it in the air with one hand. He's looking at the fingernails of the other hand. He notices the camera, brushes his little moustache, grins and, just as he drops the caravan on top of himself, the caption reads: *and Mr Stump as Mr Stump, The Strongman.*

Then the music reaches its peak and a bright-looking, scruffy-haired lad in a red Ringmaster's frockcoat that's an inch too big for him turns, faces you, grins and winks: *starring Fizzlebert Stump as Fizzlebert Stump.*

And just as you think that's the end of it (except you know it's not, because you're a fan and this is the bit you wait for before going to make a cup of tea every week) the music dwindles down to its final chords, and, out of nowhere, a honking barking noise is heard and Fizz is knocked out of the picture by the flolloping shape of a sea lion: *and introducing Fish as Fish*.

Fish honks enthusiastically, juggles a beautiful silvery sprat, winks at the camera and swallows the fish whole before letting out a burp of a remarkably smelly scent. (Luckily you can't smell it through the telly.)

The last cymbal tinkle fades away and the show (or in this case, 'the book') begins properly . . .

. . . in Chapter Two.

CHAPTER TWO

In which a boy is grumpy and in
which some children are encountered

Fizzlebert Stump, a dashing, red-headed, heroic-looking boy with a long frockcoat that once belonged to the Ringmaster flapping around his knees, jumped grumpily down the caravan steps and kicked a pebble that was lying in the grass. (The pebble hadn't done anything to deserve such a kick, but sometimes the world isn't fair.)

Let me explain quickly why he's grumpy before we get on. It won't take a moment. Fizz, the Boy Who Put His Head in the Lion's Mouth, the boy audiences loved to watch do his brave and dangerous act, the boy who took long bows every night to riotous applause, no longer bravely put his head in a dangerous lion's mouth. If you read *Fizzlebert Stump: The Boy Who Cried Fish* (probably still available from most good bookshops, several mediocre ones and the newspaper kiosk down near that bit of beach where all those jellyfish washed up last summer), you'll remember that Charles, the lion, was getting too old. He was packed away, kindly and with much love, at the end of that book to the *Twilight Tops Retirement Home* and was probably, at this very moment, sipping a tall

17

cool glass of antelope juice on a sunlounger by the pool.

Captain Fox-Dingle had replaced Charles with Kate, a friendly, if sharp-toothed crocodile, but the Boy Who Put His Head in a Crocodile's Mouth act Fizz had hoped they'd do hadn't worked out for various reasons, mostly because it was a stupid idea in the first place. So, now Fizz was without an act and, what with the Circus of Circuses show in four days' time (I'll explain that later), he was grumpy, grumbly and feeling ever so slightly sorry for himself.

Now, read on.

Fizz brushed his hair out of his eyes and began walking slowly towards some of the other caravans of his circus. He was looking for Wystan Barboozul, the bearded boy, his *sort*

of friend. It wasn't that they *weren't* friends, but they weren't the sort of friends who'd ever be *best* friends. They were too different for that. They had different interests. Fizz liked to talk about books he'd read, and Wystan liked to stick things in his beard. But they were the only two kids in the circus, and so they spent quite a lot of their time together.

This morning, however, things weren't as simple as that. Before Fizz even reached Wystan's caravan (which was actually Miss Tremble's caravan (she trained the horses)) he found his way blocked by a small crowd of people.

It was a small crowd of short people, he noticed as he got closer. And then he realised they weren't short people at all, they were other children. (Not that children aren't people: some of them definitely are, and the others should probably be included out of kindness.)

'Hey!' shouted one of the boys, in a friendly way.

'Hi,' said Fizz unenthusiastically back.

The others turned to look. There were six of them, five boys and a girl. They all looked

round about Fizz's age, give or take a few years in this or that direction.

'Wotcha,' said a second boy.

Fizz stopped walking. There was no way round them except by going through them. There were caravans on either side.

'Yeah, hi,' he mumbled. He knew what was coming. It was what he'd been worried about for the whole of the last week. It was what had made him grumpy last night. It was what had spoilt his mood over breakfast. It was what had made him kick a defenceless, innocent pebble just now. (I mentioned this a couple of pages ago. Remember?)

'Fizzlebert *Stamp*,' said a third boy, a little taller than the rest.

He had slick black hair that flopped down over one eye and a black leather jacket slung

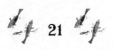

over one shoulder. He chewed his fingernails as he spoke, but not in a nervous way, just in a way that made everyone think it was cool to chew your fingernails when you spoke. He was a horrible boy, but most people didn't notice that because he mumbled and winked and clicked his fingers and that was all very cool too.

'Stump,' corrected Fizz.

'Fizzlebert *Stamp*,' repeated the lad.

Fizz sighed and said, with mock politeness, 'Good morning, Cedric *Greene*.'

Fizz had seen him once before when they were younger. Cedric was with a different circus. He did an act . . . oh, what did he do? Fizz had never seen it, but he'd heard about it. It was something to do with fire, he thought. Anyway, what Fizz *did* know was that Cedric's surname was actually *Blue*, and he was waiting for the flicker of annoyance that getting his name wrong (on purpose) would send across the older boy's face. (Just as the Stamp/Stump 'mistake' had annoyed Fizz.)

Except the older boy just said, 'Oh, you remember me? I thought you might. Good on you, *Slump*.'

He'd done it again. Look at that. And Fizz suddenly had the very real sinking feeling that the lad's name *was* Greene after all, and he'd just *thought* it was Blue because he'd been so busy trying to remember the right name but then say it wrongly that he'd probably got it muddled and had thought of the wrong name but said it rightly. Blast it.

'What do you want?' Fizz snapped, not having time for all this. (Which wasn't true, he had plenty of time.)

'What do I want?' Cedric nibbled a fingernail as he looked thoughtful. 'I want to see this famous act of yours. You and this lion.'

Fizz didn't answer, not because he couldn't think of anything to say, but because the other kids were laughing too loudly.

He hadn't met them all before, but he read the British Board of Circuses' Newsletter often enough to be able to put names to most of them (the circus world wasn't huge and every month the BBC Newsletter ran a column called 'Stars of Tomorrow' (Fizz had featured in it twice)). They all came from the other circuses Fizz's circus was parked up next to.

Besides Cedric there were four boys, none of whom looked as cool as he did, but all of whom seemed to be hanging on the leather-jacketed lad's every word, sneer and wink. Fizz

could name them all (Norman Dance, acrobat; Vincent Franklin, juggler; Abercrombie Slapdash, magician's stooge; Simon Pie, clown-in-training).

But the girl, though . . . Fizz didn't recognise her. He couldn't think of any girls he'd read about in the Newsletter who looked like her (Jemima Nail, *The Nimble Nightingale*, for instance, had long black hair (quite the opposite of this girl), and Samantha Crinkle, *The Child of Mystery*, had a nose shaped like a rabbit's drawing of a nose). Maybe she was new, or maybe she (imagine that!) didn't do an act. Whatever the case, she was listening intently to Cedric's words, just like the rest of them.

'I, um . . .' Fizz said. 'We, um . . . don't do the lion act any more.'

'No?' said Cedric, teasing the word out to silly length (sort of: 'Noo-ooo-o-o-o-ooo?').

Fizz knew that they all knew Charles had retired. Word travelled fast in the circus world (and there'd been a small article on page 2 (the back page) of the most recent BBC Newsletter), but they had to go through this game all the same.

'The way I heard it,' Cedric said, 'is that you got your head stuck and pulled all his teeth out in the middle of the show. Big-Headed Stump, that's what I hear they call you.'

'No,' Fizz said angrily, his hair bristling. 'That's not what happened.'

(It *wasn't* what happened. Not in a show. It *had* happened once in a rehearsal, but that was different; the shows had gone flawlessly right until the end.)

'Well then, the other thing I heard,' Cedric said, chewing a fingernail, the other kids hanging on his every word, 'was that it was bad breath that ended the show. I mean, there's always a *spot* of halitosis in a lion act, but when it gets so bad that . . .'

'Charles didn't—' Fizz tried to interject.

'. . . that even *the lion* complains, you know, about the boy breathing out in his mouth, about Fizzlebert *Stunk*, well, that's the end of the show.'

'How dare you?' said Fizz, standing on his tiptoes, nose to chin with Cedric. He was angry, his eyes were getting itchy and his ears were getting hot. His hands were bunching into fists at his side.

'How dare I?' Cedric said, taking a step back (but not in a cowardly way, just so they could see each other properly as he said what he was going to say). 'Do you know who you're talking to, Fizzlebert *Dump*? I'm Cedric Greene, The Boy Who Sticks His Head in the Lion's Mouth, *and*,' he paused here to let the words sink in before delivering his last, final and last words on the subject, 'I've still got a lion.'

Fizz was dumbfounded.

A second later he found himself less dumb, though still founded (whatever that means).

'I-I-I thought you did something with fire?' he stuttered.

'Used to,' Cedric said, casually. 'But fire is *so* last year. My dad bought us a lion and a new lion tamer for my birthday, because if *you're* too scared to do the act now, then I might as well give it a go, yeah? And, do you know what, *Shunt*? Even if I say so myself, I do it so much better than it's *ever* been done before. I'm a *natural*.'

'Well,' said Fizz, angrily beginning a sentence he didn't know the end of. 'Well,' he repeated, starting the sentence again in the hope it would sort itself out as it left his mouth, 'that doesn't matter, because when the people

see *my* new act, well, they'll forget all about lions and heads and mouths and stuff, because what I do now is *amazing*. Oh gosh, you'll shut up when you see what I do now.'

'I ain't heard about any new act,' said Cedric, not looking in the slightest bit concerned, just nibbling his fingernail as cool as anything.

'Well, it's secret, isn't it?' Fizz said, secretly wishing somebody had let him in on the secret too. 'It's a surprise.' You could say that again, he thought. 'You'll see on Friday.'

He hoped no one could hear the quaver in his voice that he felt vibrating with each fib he told, but it looked like the other kids had bought the story because they started muttering things like, 'Ooh, that sounds special,' and 'I wonder if it's really better than a lion,' and

'Well, we'll just have to wait and see, won't we,' until Cedric waved his hand and they fell silent.

'Stump,' he said slowly, using Fizz's real name like a threat. 'You'd better tell me what this act is right now. I don't like surprises.' He paused and looked at Fizz through squinting eyes. 'Do you know what?' he said. 'I don't think I even believe you. I reckon you're making it up.'

'I'm not.'

'Then tell me all about your brilliant new act.'

When Fizz remained silent for a second longer than he should've, Cedric turned to his friends. 'Look, he ain't got an act. He's lost his lion, and he's lied to you. Dizzybert Stimp, the most pathetic kid in the circus.'

As his cronies were slapping their sides with laughter, as Fizz could feel his cheeks burning and the rumours of frustrated, embarrassed tears welling behind his eyes, Cedric spat the nibbled edge of a fingernail high in the air where it spun in the sunlight, glinting and twirling.

The laughter stopped as every eye followed the sparkling arc of the paring (which is the technical term for the bit that comes off when you clip your nails) as it tumbled through the air above them.

Then: POW!

Cedric flew backwards through the air and landed in the dust clutching his stomach, his eyes bulging out of his face with a mix of surprise and pain.

Someone had just punched him, and, although I can't in anyway condone violence

or support it and certainly wouldn't encourage anyone reading this book to attempt to solve their problems using it, I must say, he did rather have it coming to him.

CHAPTER THREE

*In which we meet a girl called
Alice and in which we also meet a
boy called Wystan (who we've met
before, but not in this book, yet)*

Fizz looked down at his fist.

Cedric had made him mad, teasing
him like that, taunting him like that, bullying
him like that. Circuses are supposed to stick
together, not take the mickey out of each
other. Nobody could blame him for having
punched the nasty show-off.

Except . . .

Except Fizz *hadn't* punched him. His fist, while still clenched, was hanging by his side, exactly where it had been hanging before Cedric had gone flying. As far as Fizz could tell (and it was his arm, so if anyone could tell it was him) it hadn't moved at all.

He looked around.

The other kids were staring open-mouthed at where Cedric had landed, in the dust several yards away. (All except Simon Pie, the clown-in-training, who honked his horn, slapped his belly and pointed at the prone show-off, in almost exactly the way a qualified clown would do.) Now it was their turn to be struck dumb: 'But . . .' 'What . . . ?' 'Uh . . . ?'

Abercrombie Slapdash, the magician's stooge, was the first to move. He ran over to

the older boy going, 'Hey, Cedric. You alright, mate? It wasn't me.'

No, that's not quite right. He wasn't the *very* first to move. Just before he ran to help his friend, the girl, the one whose name Fizz didn't know, grabbed hold of his hand and dragged him backwards.

'Come on,' she said. 'Probably best not be here when he gets up.'

Fizz wasn't used to girls holding his hand and pulling him backwards between caravans but he quickly decided to go with the flow and followed her. (She had a very strong grip, and if he hadn't gone with her there was a possibility that when she stopped running in order to explain what was going on she'd find herself talking to a boy's arm instead of a boy. Fizz thought it best to stick together.)

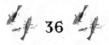

After thirty seconds' sprinting, looking over their shoulders and ducking to and fro between caravans and tents, they finally stopped.

'Oh boy,' she said, leaning on her knees to get her breath back. 'That was fun.'

Fizz stood there, his back against the back of what he recognised as Dr Surprise's caravan. (He recognised it because he saw it every day and wasn't stupid. Even though to you and me caravans probably all look pretty much the same, once you've spent time among them you soon notice the little distinguishing features. (Dr Surprise's, for example, was a subtle shade of silver not entirely unlike moonlight in the midwinter and smelt slightly waxy and had the words *Dr Surprise's Caravan* painted in large mysterious letters on the side.)) Once Fizz had got

enough breath back to form a sentence, he formed one and offered it to the girl in the shape of a question.

'What just happened?'

'We ran away, Fizzlebert Stump,' the girl said with a laugh.

'You know my name?' said Fizz.

She gave him a look that said, *Yes. Obviously.*

'But,' said Fizz, 'who are you?'

'You don't know my name?' she asked, running a hand through her hair (which was a reddish blonde and fell to just above her shoulders).

'No,' he said in a small voice.

'No reason you should. I'm Alice. Alice Crudge.'

She looked at him very closely as if she were waiting to see whether he made a joke

about her name (by singing, 'Alice look on the bright side of life,' for example) and when, after a moment, he said nothing she nodded and said, 'He deserved it, you know.'

'Who? Deserved what?' Fizz asked. For some reason his words weren't coming out as well as they normally did. His brain was a bit muddled. Alice had very blue eyes.

'That Cedric kid. He was bang out of order talking about your lion like that. So, I'm not sorry for what I did and you don't have to thank me.'

'Sorry? Thank you?'

'That's very kind of you.'

She looked away and examined her right hand, which she flexed in front of her eyes as if she were checking it still worked properly.

'You punched him?'

'Bang!' she said. 'Right in the stomach!'

'*You?*'

'Me? Yep.'

As she nodded she raised her eyebrows and pulled a face as if to say, *What a good world this is where a poor defenceless girl can stand up to bullies and give them a taste of their own medicine and then go for a healthy run so soon after*

breakfast. It was a very expressive face. It had a slightly bent nose that skewed to the left and was speckled with freckles, and a pair of fair furry eyebrows that nearly met in the middle.

'It looked like you were about to do it, and I figured *Why miss out on the fun?* And besides even an unpleasant oik like Cedric's less likely to punch a girl back.' She rocked her head from side to side and added, 'Well, the first time. But I bet he's dead angry now.' She laughed. It sounded like a shy chimpanzee falling out of a tree of medium height, but in an oddly pleasant manner.

For the second time that morning Fizz was struck dumb.

He'd been in scrapes before, been teased and bullied a bit before, he'd even been

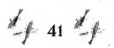

rescued before, but never by a brilliant stranger like this. *Gosh*, he thought.

'Which . . . which circus are you with?' Fizz managed to stutter. (It was an important question. Fizz's circus was one of half a dozen circuses all parked up next to one another, and some of them, such as Cedric's *A Ring & A Prayer*, were rivals of long standing with whom his Ringmaster wouldn't want him making friends.)

Alice's face lost its smile for a second and she said, '*Mumble mumble.*'

'Um? Pardon?' asked Fizz, like a dogged detective unwilling to let mumbling pass as an answer, but half mumbling his own question all the same, because he felt a little unbalanced by the person he was talking to and her blue eyes and their sudden recent bout of exercise.

'I said,' she said, '*Neil Coward's Famous Cicrus.*'

Fizz looked at her for a second, wondering if her eyes perhaps weren't quite as blue as he'd thought. Then he shook his head. It didn't matter that her circus was the circus other circuses laughed at behind the back of its Medium Top (a Big Top was too big for *Neil Coward's Famous Cicrus* (and money was so tight they had never been able to afford to repaint the name on the side of their lorry to correct the spelling mistake that's already upsetting my editor, Kate, who likes things to be spelt properly in these books)). *Coward's* was the place acts ended up when they'd run out of talent, luck or custard. But Fizz couldn't hold it against Alice, could he? It wasn't her fault, she just had to live where her parents lived. That's the way it goes.

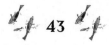

After all, he knew she wasn't rubbish, was she? She'd just sort of rescued him.

He gave her a smile and was about to ask her what she did, what her act was, when a thin wavering voice interrupted him.

'Fizzlebert Stump?'

For half a second he thought it was Cedric back for more, but then he looked up and saw Dr Surprise's head sticking out the caravan above him.

'Dr Surprise,' Fizz said, finding his words at last. 'I'm down here.'

'I knew that,' the Doctor replied. He was, in case you didn't know, the circus's mind reader, hypnotist, illusionist and general go-to man for magic and mystery (and history lessons (and rabbit-related facts (and carrots))). 'But, you see, Wystan didn't.'

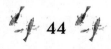

'Didn't what?' asked Fizz, confusedly.

'Know you were down there. He was just here, looking for you. At that point I didn't know you were here either, because you weren't. It was only after he'd gone that I heard the thud of your arrival.' (The two of them had stopped running quite suddenly, when they hit the caravan.) 'It made Flopples jump, Fizzlebert. I had to calm her with an extra soothing between-meals carrot.' The Doctor paused and thought about it. 'She is a rabbit, though, and they are meant to have a little jump every now and then, so no harm done, eh?'

'Where is he now?' Fizz asked, interrupting Dr Surprise before he went off on a long lecture about Flopples' likes and dislikes.

'Oh, Fizzlebert, I am surprised at you,' the Doctor said. 'Not "he" but "she". And she's

right here on my bed, chewing the blanket and dreaming sweet dreams. As I said, she's quite recovered from the shock –'

'No, I meant Wystan. Where's Wystan now?'

'I don't know,' said Dr Surprise. 'What am I? Some sort of mind reader?'

Fizz looked at the Doctor, raised an eyebrow and said nothing.

'Okay. Yes,' the Doctor agreed, reading Fizz's mind, 'I *am* some sort of a mind reader and I think he was going back to his caravan to pick something up before resuming the search for you. So maybe he's there.'

'Thanks, Dr Surprise,' Fizz said as the Doctor vanished back inside the caravan.

'Who's this Wystan?' asked Alice.

'Oh, he's just a boy I know. Lives in my circus,' Fizz said. 'He's a bit . . . hairy.'

'Well, if he's looking for you, let's go find him first.'

That seemed a sensible plan to Fizz. He could show his new friend off to his old friend. (*Was* she his new friend? She seemed friendly and was certainly new. Wystan would be very jealous.)

Wystan wasn't very jealous. In fact, when they tracked him down to just outside Miss Tremble's caravan, he was so eager to tell Fizz his news that he didn't even ask who the feisty red-headed bent-nosed bully-basher was.

'Fizz,' he gabbled instead. 'Something brilliant's happened! Something amazing!'

This was odd, this enthusiasm, because Wystan was normally a quiet lad, a bit dour maybe, you might even say grumpy (which was one of the reasons he sometimes got on Fizz's nerves). It made a change to see him so excited.

'What is it?' Fizz asked.

'It's me mum and dad,' Wystan replied. 'I don't think they're dead after all. I've seen them! This morning!'

His beard wobbled excitedly as he spoke. Fizz noticed that Wystan had had cornflakes for breakfast, and not just any old cornflakes, but the special ones with nuts stuck to them.

'But . . .' Fizz said, beginning a sentence he wasn't sure he knew how to end.

(I should probably insert a word of explanation at this point. When Wystan Barboozul first appeared at Fizz's circus (an appearance recounted in a book aptly called *Fizzlebert Stump and the Bearded Boy* (a book *also* probably still available in some good bookshops, a few rubbish ones and that place Keith runs at the side of his house which mainly sells spare parts for train sets)) he was accompanied by a pair of not-parents, Lord and Lady Barboozul, who turned out to be . . .well, I don't want to spoil it for anyone who's not read that book

yet, but let's just say, 'They turned out to be . . .' and add that Wystan was left behind in the care of the circus.

The reason he was with *them* was that they'd been left in charge of him after his parents had died, or more specifically (as mentioned in Chapter Three of the aforementioned (or 'previouslysaid' which is a word I just made up meaning the same as 'aforementioned' but am not allowed to use on account of having just made it up) volume) after they'd gone missing, presumed dead.

Since that book he'd lived under the protection of Fizz's circus, in the caravan of Miss Tremble and her horses (although, to tell you the truth, the horses were only allowed in the caravan for special occasions (birthdays, Christmas, weekends, heavy rain), and even then only ever two at a time. More often they spent their time outside in a portable paddock.)

Fizz was naturally surprised at the sudden and unexpected news of Wystan's parents' sudden and unexpected reappearance. He tried to imagine how it might feel to find your mum and dad again after you'd believed, for years, that they were gone forever. How strange it must be. How odd a feeling. His stomach was twirling just thinking about it, and he knew that he couldn't really share a hundredth of the real excitement Wystan must have been bubbling with inside.

During the months that Wystan had been in the circus Fizz had only ever once or twice been in his bedroom (Miss Tremble's caravan was pretty big, having *two* bedrooms *plus* a place for hanging hay bales). Next to his bed Wystan had a photo of his parents in a little frame. At least, Fizz had assumed they were his bearded companion's parents because of the moustaches and the tiny bearded baby one of them held in his arms, but when Wystan had seen him look at it he'd coughed into his beard, pointed out the window, knocked the picture face down and changed the subject.

But now there was no need for Wystan to be embarrassed about his dead parents any more because they weren't dead any more. That was great news.

But, Fizz suddenly thought, why wasn't he with them? Where were they?

'Why aren't you with them?' he asked. 'Where are they?'

'Ah,' Wystan said, coughing and lowering his beard shyly. 'Well, I've not actually been up and said "Hello" or nothing.'

'Why not?' Alice asked.

Wystan seemed to notice her for the first time. He looked her up and down and frowned as if he wasn't impressed with what he saw.

'Fizz,' Wystan said, turning back and twirling his whiskers not like a villain might do, but like a little boy who was scared of something lurking in the dark. 'I'm nervous. What if they don't want me?'

'Why wouldn't they want you?' Alice asked.

'It's been years,' the bearded boy replied, not really looking at her. 'I was just a baby when they went missing. How come they never came looking? How come they left me with the Barboozuls for so long?'

'I'm sure there's a perfectly ordinary explanation,' Fizz said, without offering an example, because he couldn't think of one right there and then (although he was sure if you gave him long enough he'd be able to come up with something).

'Where were they?' Alice asked. 'You know, when you saw them?'

'Did they see you?' Fizz asked.

'They were over by the Big Big Top,' Wystan replied. 'I reckon they work there. But I don't think they saw me . . .'

'Well,' Fizz began. 'We'd best go find them.'

'No,' said Wystan. 'I don't want to.'

Fizz looked at his friend and scratched his head.

'You have to,' he said. 'It's the right thing to do.'

'I'm . . . I'm scared.'

'But, Wystan, you've been juggled by a sea lion, attacked by a shark, hurled through the air by elastic beards. You stood up to Lord and Lady Barboozul, you've wrestled a koala, you've done a triple beardflip from the high wire and landed in a blancmange.' (Not all of these happened in books I've written, but some of them did.) 'How can you be scared of *this*? How can *you* be scared of your *mum and dad*?'

Wystan said nothing, but tugged at his beard in a way that said, 'Yes, but . . .'

'Okay,' Fizz said and he looked at Alice. She smiled (her eyebrows met when she smiled, it was odd but oddly cute) and nodded.

She took hold of Wystan's left arm and Fizz took hold of his right and, without a

word, they frogmarched him off in the direction of the Big Big Top. (Frogs, it should be said, are rubbish at marching, and so was Wystan. A more accurate description would be 'frog-half-dragged-and-half-pulled', and, to be honest, we could probably do without the frog bit entirely. And when I said 'without a word' that just meant Fizz and Alice were silent. Wystan, for his part, gave voice to a number of rude and rudeish words which were fortunately muffled by his beard so that you don't have to hear them.)

I realise we've got this far, by the way, with all these revelations and these new characters popping up all over the place without me even telling you where the circus had parked up for the book. I mean, anyone with even a

rudimentary grasp of circus life would have been wondering why on earth there are all these other circuses hanging around. When a circus stops in a town to put on its show, it's usually the *only* circus in town. Circuses don't often meet other circuses, so this does all seem a bit weird.

Trust me though, I'll explain everything in the next chapter, along with giving you the first glimpse of Wystan's parents (if that's who they really are) and some further discoveries about this exciting new girl on the scene, Alice Crudge. Trust me, I'm not a doctor.

CHAPTER FOUR

In which some moustaches are met
and in which an act is interrupted

Wystan had quickly given in to the plan. He wasn't happy about it, but the other two weren't having to drag him any more, although he was still managing to drag his feet all by himself.

And then there, in a little gaggle of circus folk, by the Big Big Top's backstage flap they saw them: Wystan's parents.

Fizzlebert recognised them instantly. He didn't need the bearded boy to point them out. There were only two people in that little crowd who looked like the people in Wystan's photograph.

The man was wearing plain blue overalls and had short brown hair and a big curling aviator's moustache. Of course, he also had a nose and eyes and ears and all the usual bits as well, but it was the moustache Fizz recognised (even though he'd only seen the photo once, months before, it had stuck in his mind). The woman, on the same hand, was also wearing blue overalls and had short brown hair and a big curling aviator's moustache. Like the man she had all the rest of the normal features, naturally, but Fizz's eyes were drawn back, time and again, to her moustache. The

way it matched the man's, but pointed down where his pointed up, was quite uncanny. She definitely looked a bit like the woman in Wystan's photo. (The bit being, mainly, the moustache.) If these *were* his parents then it was clear where he got his hairy genes from (and I don't mean furry trousers, as you well knew, so it was silly to even think I might have been thinking about making a joke at a time like this).

They were about to go into the tent. Mr Gomez, the farmer, had just gone in and they were following, but Fizz ran over and shouted for them to stop.

'Mr and Mrs Barboozul,' he said. 'Have I got a surprise for you!'

They stopped and looked at the excitable boy.

'I'm sorry?'

'Look,' Fizz said, as Alice pushed Wystan in front of her, 'it's Wystan!'

'Wystan who?' asked the woman.

'Wystan Barboozul. Your son.'

The woman looked at the man and then they both looked at Wystan.

'I don't remember having one of those,' the man said.

'Of course you do,' Fizz said. 'He was a baby when your balloon got blown off course. You went missing.'

'Oh, we've not gone missing,' said the woman. 'We're right here.'

'But before,' Fizz said. 'You went missing before.'

'I don't remember that,' the man said, stroking his moustache.

There was a shout from inside the tent.

'Where are you two?' called Mr Gomez, sticking his head through the flap. 'We've got judging to do.'

'Oh hello,' said the woman.

'Come on,' said Gomez. 'Quickly. Chop chop.'

Without looking back the pair who looked exactly like Wystan's parents followed the farmer into the Big Top. The three kids were left tapping the grass with their feet out the back.

'Why didn't you say anything?' Fizz asked.

'It wouldn't do no good,' Wystan said, gloomily. 'You saw them. They don't know who I am. They didn't recognise me.'

'But maybe if you'd just said "Hello!" even . . .' Fizz began, wondering if that would

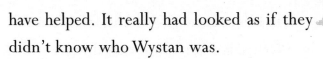

have helped. It really had looked as if they didn't know who Wystan was.

'Are they them?' Alice asked.

Wystan nodded.

'I'm sure of it. That's them, and they don't want me.'

'No,' Alice said. 'It's not that, I don't reckon. I think they've got amnesia.'

'Of course!' Fizz shouted, 'That's it. Oh, Alice! You're brilliant.'

She took a bow.

'What's "amnesia"?' Wystan asked, chewing the corner of his beard.

'You don't know?' Fizz said, sounding slightly surprised because it was the sort of thing that was always happening to people in books he read.

'I did know,' Wystan said, slowly, 'but I've forgotten.'

Fizz laughed and slapped his friend on the beard, thinking he was making a joke.

Alice coughed gently and Fizz looked at Wystan's face. It wasn't an I-just-made-a-joke sort of face.

'Oh,' he said, trying to sound as if he hadn't just slapped his friend's beard and laughed. 'Amnesia is when you forget everything. They must've hit their heads or something, and have forgotten all about you.'

Wystan gave a big sigh which rustled through his beard like a sorrowful autumn wind through a leafless (but furry) weeping willow.

'Well, that's that then,' he said, definitely not tearfully (unless you looked really close, but that would be rude, so we won't). 'Nothing to be done.'

Before Fizz could reach out to stop him, or say 'No it isn't, there's loads we can do to make them remember you, Wystan Barboozul, the Bearded Boy and expert acrobat', he had run off.

'Come on,' Fizz said. 'Let's go get him.'

Alice caught hold of his arm and said, 'Don't be daft. He wants to have a blub. Look at him, he's all upset, and so would you be too. You gotta give him some space. Give him some time.'

Fizz saw the wisdom of her words. They just added to his growing feeling that this bent-nosed, red-haired girl was . . . well, what? He didn't want to think exactly what it was she was, rather, he just believed it was probably good.

'Let's go see what's on,' Alice said, grabbing his hand and pulling him into the cool dark of the Big Big Top.

Fizz looked around the stalls and saw a few people sat about the place waiting to watch that morning's acts. There probably weren't more than a dozen of them. Most of the other circus folk were busy rehearsing, practising or adding final, extra tricks to their already wonderful acts.

The Big Big Top was the biggest Big Top he'd seen. It was much bigger than his circus's one. Forgetting Wystan's problems for the moment, Fizz felt his heart race. Oh, if only he could get to perform in there on Saturday night. Imagine the crowd! Thousands of them all watching him as he . . .

Well? As he did what? Pretended to put his head in a pretend lion's mouth? His heart sank. He'd been searching for days for a new act. Something he was good at, that would

make him a star again. But so far, nothing. If only he could turn that *nothing* into a *something*. How hard could it be?

His heart sank further, knocking his stomach to one side as it plunged towards the ground. He couldn't help but remember the promise he'd made to Cedric, the challenge he'd thrown out, the words he'd said in the heat of the moment. Not only did he need to work up a new act for himself, for his own sake, but he also had to do it to stop that leather-jacketed bully, that smug show-off, that boy-who-said-he-had-a-lion from being such a smug, lion-owning, leather-jacketed bully.

If Friday came and he had no act . . . well, he'd never be able to show his face again. He'd be crushed.

He wasn't much cheered when Alice said, 'Look!' She was pointing at the clowns who were warming up nearby. 'There's one of them kids that was teasing you.'

It was Simon Pie, clown-in-training. He'd painted his face since we last saw him back in Chapter Two. It was now chalk white with big sad red lips. He wore the blue nose of a student clown.

Fizz sniffed and looked away, only to see three figures settling themselves down behind a table at the edge of the sawdust ring.

One of the figures was Mr Gomez, the farmer, a huge roundish shape, much like the vegetables he grew (I'll tell you about those in a minute), with a fuzzy grey stubble over his chin and dark glasses over his eyes. And beside him, one sat either side, were the two

moustachioed amnesiac-Wystan-parents. *They must be his fellow judges*, Fizz thought.

It was only later on, after he'd spent a little more time with them, that Fizz wondered exactly how two such forgetful people could judge anything, but by then he had a good idea that Mr Gomez wasn't big on taking advice and that they were in fact his ideal fellow judges.

Actually now would probably be a good time, while Fizz and Alice watch Simon Pie and his fellow clowns go through their act, to explain exactly what's going on with all these circuses and this farmer chap.

To begin at the beginning, Mr Gomez's farm wasn't the biggest of farms. It had seven medium-sized fields in which he grew those odd-shaped things you sometimes see in the vegetable section of supermarkets but which you don't know the name of and which you never see anyone buying. In the middle of the fields was his farmhouse, where he spent most of his time looking out the window and wondering what his vegetables were called.

Come the autumn, when the last of his odd-shaped stock was sent off to the shops and before the next year's crop had been sown, he opened his fields up to a different sort of farming. You might call it circus farming. (When he was a boy his father had known a man whose brother had married a woman whose uncle worked in a circus (he swept the sawdust), and this had planted in Mr Gomez's heart a lifelong love of all things circussy.)

For more years than he could count on a small abacus this *Gathering* (as they called it) had happened. The way it worked was this: in one of the seven fields he put up the Big Big Top, and in the others six specially invited circuses parked up. Then, over the course of a week, he saw all the acts from the six circuses, picked the very best ones and on Saturday night put on a show in the Big Top to which he sold tickets and invited the local press. It was usually filmed by a chap from Austrian television (or was it Australian television? Mr Gomez could never remember what the difference was, but they paid well for the privilege so he didn't ask).

He called it 'The Circus Of Circuses' and, even though he was just a farmer, the British Board of Circuses had smiled upon him and given him an 'Official Honorary Member of the BBC' certificate and a special badge he could wear during the Gathering. The BBC published a big glossy supplement with lots of photos of the Circus of Circuses show with a full list of acts in the Christmas edition of their official newsletter and anyone who was anyone, naturally, wanted to be in it (because they could send copies to their friends and family instead of having to write and

photocoy those tedious letters saying things like '*This year the Algebra family had a smashing time. Little Timmy went surfing in Cornwall with Mr Pickles who lives next door and Maisie caught cat flu from Mr Pickles who lives next door ...*' that dreadful adults like to send to each other in their Christmas cards).

What I'm saying is that, even though (as I've said several times) Mr Gomez was just a farmer, the Circus of Circuses show was a Big Deal in the circus world. For Fizz's circus to be among the six that had been invited to compete this year had made their Ringmaster swell with pride. (Mrs Needlethrust, the circus's nurse, had made him swallow a week's worth of anti-inflammatory pills to counter-act the swelling, even though he'd tried to explain to her that it was just a metaphor.

'Nasty things, metaphors,' she'd said, doubling the dose.)

Now, back to Fizzlebert . . .

Out in the ring half a dozen clowns were going through their routine, pouring custard in one another's trousers, 'accidentally' knocking each other down with ladders they were carrying for no reason at all and pointing at other peoples' misfortune. So far so normal. But then Simon Pie picked up a bucket from the side of the ring and threw it at the Chief Clown (he had the biggest bow tie, almost twice the size of his head, that's how you knew he was the boss). Fizz expected yet more custard or whitewash or sparkly tinsel (which clowns use when they've got a volunteer from the audience (it gives them the experience of being

attacked by a clown armed with a bucket of
water or custard, but with none of the cleaning bills)), but what emerged was none of the
usual things. It was fish.

Oh, sure, there was *some* custard involved,
but the custard was full of silvery fish-shaped
things which Fizz, from a long familiarity,
immediately recognised as being the silvery fish-shaped things that fish experts call
'fish'.

That the fish weren't part of the act became
apparent from what happened next.

The Chief Clown, picking mackerel out
of his clothes, started shouting at little Simon
Pie (not using usual clown words either, but
a whole different set of non-clown words
that you won't find in the dictionaries they
keep in school but which you might hear on a

late-night television programme about Hell's Angels).

Simon stood stock still in shock and gingerly looked inside the bucket (which was now empty) as if he might find a note written on the bottom of it explaining what had just happened. Finding nothing, he began to cry.

There are few things sadder than seeing a clown-in-training cry, his tears leaving pink streaks down his cheeks where the face paint was stripped away.

Few things are *sadder*, but I think some things are *funnier*.

For example, six sea lions attacking a custard-and-fish-covered Chief Clown from six different directions at once. That would be pretty funny, yes? Well, I'm sorry to say most circuses don't have a resident sea lion (they're

capricious animals (technically, 'capricious' means 'having a head like a hedgehog' (go look it up: as unlikely as it sounds I speak the truth) but here it just means moody or unpredictable ('prickly', if you like))), and so the Chief Clown was only attacked by one, Fish. (Not, as you might think if someone's reading this out loud, by *one fish* but by *one sea lion called Fish*. Obviously.)

This is how it happened: first Mr Gomez looked at the glass of water beside his notes on the table. He looked around the ring to see if anyone else had noticed it. He looked back. There were circular ripples appearing in the water. Regular, like a heartbeat. Something was coming this way. Then he felt a rumbling in the ground. Clowns began to look this way and that. Then the sawdust in the ring began

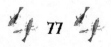

to shake in the air. The Chief Clown stopped shouting at poor Simon and looked towards the main flapway where a slim shaft of sunlight could be seen. There was a noise from out there, from outside, a noise like distant thunder, coming closer. And then, through the flaps, burst a flolloping shape, dark, streamlined, toothy, smelly (both in the sense of ponging a bit of fish and also sniffing loudly at the air) and ever so hungry.

Fish, Fizz knew, could smell fish from a mile and a half away and when he'd not eaten in the last seven minutes (or so) was drawn to a new fishy scent like a magnet to a bar of chocolate (a metal bar of chocolate, obviously).

The Chief Clown was knocked to the ground as Fish landed on top of him, gobbling mackerel and sardines from where they'd

fallen. Then, when all the loose fish were gone, the sea lion began rummaging inside the clown's clothes for any strays.

If a sea lion attacking a clown is funnier than a crying clown-in-training, then a Chief Clown screaming with fear at the snapping jaws of a rogue sea lion inside his voluminous silken custardy trousers is simply troubling. I'd look the other way if I were you.

'Fish!' Fizz shouted, climbing over the railing in between the seating and the ring. There was no one else from his circus there and he felt, somewhat, somehow, sort of, responsible for Fish's actions. (Or at the very least he thought someone was going to make a fuss about this (probably the Chief Clown) and if they knew Fizz had been there and had done nothing they'd include him in the fuss.)

Fish wasn't finished yet and the Chief Clown was still wriggling and writhing in the sawdust.

Mr Gomez and the two moustachioed judges were watching with interest and taking notes. Every now and then they whispered to one another. A crowd of fearful clowns had formed around their Chief and were gently, vaguely considering thinking about possibly one day poking at the sea lion with their long shoes, but they were too scared.

Fizz was pushing at his nautical friend. 'Come on,' he was saying. 'Get off him.' But it wasn't working. Fish was too heavy for him to move. Even Fizz (who had a Strongman for a father) couldn't shift a hungry sea lion who didn't want to move.

And then Alice appeared at his side.

'He with you?' she said, nodding at Fish.

'Yes,' said Fizz. 'I'm afraid so. He's a bit of a nuisance . . .'

But before he could say anything else Alice had reached over and lifted Fish up and off the Chief Clown, who immediately stopped screaming and began honking his emergency horn and shouting something about 'the sea, the sea'.

'Shall we get out of here?' she asked, holding Fish casually under her arm, like you or I might carry a large cat or a small dog, or a normal-sized sea lion if you or I were strong enough.

Fizz looked around at the angry clown crowd and nodded.

They strolled as calmly, as coolly, and as collectedly as they could out of the Big Top.

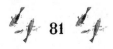

Fish was silent as they walked, just looking around hopefully, assuming there would be more fish at the end of the journey, and burping fishily with each jiggle.

'Wow,' said Fizz when they'd got out into the fresh air. 'You're really strong.'

Alice lifted Fish above her head and shrugged her shoulders (which sounds a weird thing to do, as if it wouldn't work, but it's perfectly possible, because she did it).

'Yeah, I suppose,' she said. 'My grand-dad was a Strongman. I guess it runs in the family.'

'So is that what you do?' he asked.

Fish honked excitedly. From up there he could see a duck pond.

'I wish,' Alice began, 'but –'

Before she could finish her sentence a man came running over, shouting.

'Alice!' he shouted as he ran. 'Alice Crudge! Put that thing down at once. Put it down. What will people think?'

Alice put Fish down gently and he waddled away, leaving behind the smell of kippers, smoked salmon and spangly waistcoat.

'Dad,' Alice sighed. 'I was just –'

'I don't want to hear it, young lady,' her father said, cutting her off. He was a short man with a flowery haircut and a shirt that tried to outdo Christmas for sparkles. For someone who looked so colourful, he seemed remarkably sour. 'We've been looking for you all morning. Your mother's sick with worry. You need to be rehearsing. You've got to be perfect. We can't have you letting us down again. Now come on home.'

He turned around, completely ignoring Fizzlebert, and flounced off, obviously expecting his daughter to follow.

'I've gotta go,' she said, glumly. 'I've gotta rehearse.'

'Weightlifting?' Fizz asked, knowing how often his father had to practise to keep his

muscles in tiptop condition, to keep the act fresh, always trying to lift something a little bit heavier or a different colour than the last thing.

'Flerrajin,' Alice mumbled, running off. 'Sorry,' she added, giving Fizz a sad smile over her shoulder.

Fizz stood and watched her go until he was alone outside the Big Top, until even the smell of fish/Fish had vanished.

He pondered what she'd just said.

He rolled the strange word round and round in his head until the sounds of it fell into place and made the noise of something that seemed to make sense, except it didn't make sense at all.

'Flower Arranging?' he said out loud.

He was busy thinking, his brain buzzing with questions. Firstly, why was a girl as

strong as Alice doing a Flower Arranging act? Secondly, how could they get Wystan's parents (if that was who they were, and it looked like it was) to remember him? Thirdly, someone had put those fish in Simon Pie's bucket: who? And fourthly and finally, Fizz still needed to learn a new act in order to be in with a chance of being picked for the Circus of Circuses show on Saturday night and to show Cedric that he wasn't a loser and so on and so forth.

Goodness but it's busy inside Fizz's head. I think we've all earned a break.

CHAPTER FIVE

In which some acts are tried on for
size and in which a plan is plotted

When Fizz found Wystan, later that
morning, the bearded boy was quiet
and grumpy and didn't say anything about what
had happened earlier on, but Fizz hadn't really
expected anything else. He told Wystan that he
had to get his mum and dad back and to do that
he'd have to get them to remember him. Wystan
grumbled but Fizz told him he had a plan. Fizz

told him that he knew who they should talk to. Fizz told him that everything would be alright. (Fizz was being very decisive, other people's problems being easier to be decisive about than one's own.) Wystan grumbled even more, but agreed to listen to Fizz's plan because if he didn't, he knew Fizz would tell him it anyway.

Naturally, I won't tell you what Fizz's plan actually was because I don't believe in listening in to other people's conversations. It's rude, and if there's one thing I never am it's rude. You can ask anyone. Well, not *anyone*, obviously, but anyone who knows me. (Except Abigail Bigginshaw because she's an idiot who doesn't know what she's talking about.)

Anyway, the next thing Wystan knew, he and Fizz were having lunch in the circus's Mess Tent, sat opposite Dr Surprise.

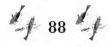

'Doctor,' Fizz said. 'We've got a problem.'

'Oh?' said Dr Surprise, poking a carrot under his top hat.

'Wystan's found his mum and dad, but they've forgotten him.'

'Oh?' said Dr Surprise, removing a carrot stump from under his top hat.

'We reckon they've got amnesia.'

'That would explain the forgetfulness,' said the Doctor.

'I thought you might know how to get their memories back. I mean you're the doctor here.' Fizz thought for a moment. 'And the mind reader.' Another moment. 'And the hypnotist.'

Dr Surprise nodded his head slowly at each statement. There was no way he could argue with the description. Fizz knew him too well.

'Yes,' he said.

Wystan, who'd been looking anxious (or as anxious as a boy can look behind such a big beard (if you'd not met him before you'd have the feeling of being watched by someone from behind a small brown bush)), mumbled something. It hadn't been his idea to ask Dr Surprise for help.

'Speak up,' said Fizz, nudging him in the beard.

'Can you help?' Wystan grumbled.

'Oh no,' Dr Surprise said, sounding startled. 'No, I don't think that would be right. I think when people have forgotten things they tend to forget them for good reasons. Why, I met an old man once who had been in the French Foreign Legion. He'd hated it. Turned out he was allergic to camels. And sand. And sunshine. I met him in a hut just outside Aberdeen where he'd been living for twenty years as a hermit. I'd heard he was the only person who still remembered how to perform Finnegan's Wave, a glorious illusion I'd read about in *Smith's Muddled Arcana*, the foremost book of –'

Fizz interrupted with a cough, to which he added a, 'But, Doctor, what about Wystan's mum and dad?'

'What I was saying, Fizzlebert, if you'd let me finish, was that this chap had become a hermit in order to forget about the Foreign Legion, and he had managed to almost entirely forget it. He'd also forgotten the trick. I tried to jog his memory and he got very upset with me.'

Dr Surprise began to roll up his trouser leg.

'But, Doctor, what has all that to do with us?'

'A scar, Fizzlebert. Look, a scar.'

The Doctor pointed at his leg.

'I don't dabble in memories,' he said. 'That's all. It's too dangerous.'

Wystan stuffed the end of his beard in his mouth and muttered.

'Well,' said the Doctor, seeing how important it was to the boy. 'I'll tell you what. Rather than upset them, I could have a word with Mr Gomez. He might be able to shed some light on the situation. They're probably not your parents, Wystan. There are lots of moustaches in the world.' He took his off and gave it a polish (he had a collection of them from Christmas crackers (good-quality crackers, mind you)). 'This is probably just a case of mistaken identity. But I will ask for you.'

With that the Doctor stood up, stuck a handful of carrots in one pocket and a small

bowl of ice cream in the other, and left the Mess Tent.

'I think that went quite well,' said Fizz, not believing a word of it.

'No harm done,' Wystan mumbled gloomily. 'But I'm still stuck where I am.'

Fizzlebert had a thought.

'Have you shown them the photograph?'

'What photograph?'

'The one by your bed.'

Wystan looked cross (as cross as a boy can look over the top of a big beard, as mentioned before).

'How did you know about –'

'It was an accident,' Fizz said quickly. 'I saw it once, by accident.'

Wystan scrunched the edge of his beard in his hand.

'Well, okay,' he said.

'Have you?'

'No.'

'Worth a try?'

Wystan shrugged.

There were trials of one act after another going on in the Big Big Top all afternoon. Wystan wouldn't be able to get close to his folks before the evening, when they all broke for dinner. He told Fizz he was going to spend the afternoon rehearsing with Fish (they did acrobatics together). Fizz on the other hand spent his afternoon searching for an act that would let him join.

He went from caravan to caravan knocking on doors and asking if anyone needed an extra hand.

As dispiriting afternoons go, this one was a winner. As winning afternoons go, on the other hand, this one was dispiriting.

Emerald Sparkles, the knife thrower, threw knives at her husband as he spun round on a big wooden wheel. The trick was that the knives didn't hit him, but stuck in the wood of the wheel next to him. It was a very impressive act, and would have been even more impressive if she wasn't on her fourth husband.

Fizz didn't volunteer to be a target (or non-target, as it were), but wondered politely if she needed someone to hand her the knives. He thought he could do that in a suave and sophisticated manner. He wouldn't say anything, just look dashing in his ex-Ringmaster's coat.

They didn't need him.

William and Bill Clubs, the circus's favourite juggling brother combo, were intrigued by the idea of adding a new little brother into the act, but when they threw their flaming sticks at Fizz he yelped, leapt aside and set fire (briefly) to their tent. They decided to pass on his offer.

He visited the Two Robbies. These were two grown men, one called Robert and one called Robin, who dressed up in cardboard boxes, painted themselves silver and did a robo-dancing turn. How hard, Fizz wondered, could that be to do?

It turned out he was allergic to tin foil.

Abelard Pratt (of *Abelard Pratt and his Swinging Cat* fame) wouldn't let Fizz help with his act. It was rather a specialised act which involved him entering a series of rooms of decreasing size (skilfully erected in the ring by his glamorous assistant Dave) in which he swung a series of increasingly small cats in tighter circles. Exactly why the Ringmaster allowed this act in his circus was a matter of some debate (the debate usually

centring on whether it was due to blackmail or a bet).

No cat had been harmed, and everyone had to agree Abelard Pratt was very good at what he did, but that was hardly the point.

Pratt had no need of Fizz in his act but did have a suggestion.

'Fizzle,' he said in a creepy creeping accent which might have been Transylvanian, Dutch or Bristolian, 'you are the boy who did things to a lion, yes?'

'Yes, sort of,' Fizz said.

'You put your head in the big cat's mouth part, am I right?'

'Yes,' Fizz agreed again.

'Well,' Pratt continued as if having a brainwave, 'I lend you a loan of my Samantha, a kitten with whom I am training at the

moment. Hasn't learnt to duck. But for you she will be beautiful.'

'Yes?'

'Yes, no longer will you be *Fizzle Stump: The Boy Who Puts His Head in a Lion's Mouth Part*. No. Now you will have new act. It will be *Samantha Cat: The Kitten Who Puts Her Head in a Boy's Mouth Part*. Turn tables, yes? No one will have seen such an act. Will be famous again!'

It sounded good, but Fizz knew it would upset Captain Fox-Dingle to see him working with another cat so soon after . . . The Captain missed his lion. They'd been together for years.

Reluctantly, he realised he had to say, 'No,' to Abelard Pratt. What had he been thinking? *Thoughtless Fizz*, Fizz thought.

He went to see Apology Cheesemutter. Apology wasn't his real name, but he said 'sorry' so often that after a week in the circus the nickname had stuck. Nobody remembered what it had replaced. He wasn't really called Cheesemutter either, but he went on about cheese a lot under his breath, so after another week in the circus that nickname had stuck too. No one remembered what this one had replaced either.

Cheesemutter trained mice. They were very special mice. Because the arena in which a circus performer must perform is quite large and because there are no big video screens to relay to the people in the back row what it is they can't quite see down in the ring, normal-size mice doing normal-size tricks would be rather pointless. So Apology Cheesemutter had

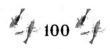

got himself some giant mice. (I must be very clear about this because some of the people reading this book are probably quite intelligent and are saying to themselves, 'Giant mice? You mean he trained some rats?' But Cheesemutter hadn't trained a bunch of rats and called them mice, that would have been fraudulent (which is the same thing as being a liar, which he wasn't). What Cheesemutter had instead done was stick mouse ears on some dogs and called *them* mice (or as everyone else called them, 'mice').)

Cheesemutter was happy to let Fizz help out with the 'mice'. He gave him a piece of cheese on a string and showed him how to pull it through and across a sort of obstacle course of hoops and seesaws and fences that the 'mice' would negotiate, the cheese-flavoured treat on their mind.

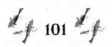

There was only one problem: dogs (by which I mean 'mice') don't like cheese (and please don't say, 'But *our* dog loves cheese,' or 'My auntie Jean has a dog which likes nothing more than a chunk of Cheddar,' or 'I was rescued from an avalanche once by a St Bernard that refused to go away until I'd given him my cheese and pickle sandwich,' because I don't care about all that. The only thing that's important is that Apology Cheesemutter's dogs ('mice') didn't like cheese, which is one of the reasons he muttered about it so much, and possibly also one of the reasons he apologised so often).

Fizz pulled the cheese-laden string through a slalom of poles watched by a German shepherd (who annoyingly kept saying, 'Schnell,' which means 'Faster' in German). Eventually

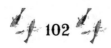

Cheesemutter asked him to move his sheep since they were distracting the 'mice'.

It was a few minutes after the man had moved on and Fizz's 'mouse' had made no effort to chase the cheese for the twenty-fourth time that a different voice, one he'd hoped not to hear ever again, broke his concentration.

'So, *Scrimp*, moved on to dogs, have we? This looks a *brilliant* act.' That was sarcasm. 'Dogs that do impressions of stuffed dead things. I bet this gets the audience on their feet.' Cedric Greene paused meaningfully, before delivering his punchline, '*Leaving*.'

He spat a bit of fingernail as he said the last word and followed it with a wicked laugh.

'They're not dogs,' Fizz said, feeling as stupid as he sounded (but Apology

Cheesemutter was sensitive and no one ever said the 'D' word around him, just in case he began crying again). 'They're "mice".'

Cedric looked at the pair of mouse ears glued to a headband that the poodle was wearing and frowned.

'Whatever,' he said, brushing the oddness aside with a long-fingered hand.

'Anyway,' Fizz said, his stomach bubbling inside him, his heart beating loud in his mouth, 'this isn't my act, I'm just helping out for a friend. That's what we do in our circus, we help each other out.'

'So, you still not going to tell me what this brilliant new act of yours *really* is, then?'

'No,' said Fizz. 'It's a surprise.'

You didn't have to be a mind reader to see that Cedric didn't believe a word Fizz was

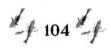

saying. He thought Fizz was just making it up to save face, and although you know and I know that he was right, that doesn't make it any better. He was smug and unpleasant and even though he just happened to be right, I wouldn't let it count in his favour.

'Alright then,' he said, slowly and with a big grin. 'I reckon maybe we should have a little wager.'

'What?'

'A bet. On who has the best act. On whose act Gomez picks for the big show. On whose act is simply the most wonderful.'

'A bet?'

'Yes, Fizzlebert *Schlump*, a wager.' He leant closer to Fizz, so our hero could smell his chewing gum. 'Do you read the British Board of Circuses Newsletter?'

'Yes, of course. Everyone does.'

'The letters page. The loser has to write a letter to the editor saying that I, Cedric Greene, am the best juvenile act in the whole country, that only I deserve the right to be the Boy Who Puts His Head in the Lion's Mouth, and that I do it better than you ever did.'

Fizz gulped. *Everyone* read the newsletter, everyone in the circus world anyway. The Ringmaster read bits out during his motivational speeches. Dr Surprise used it to line the bottom of Flopples' cage. His parents had a scrapbook with family cuttings in, every mention a Stump (or Flange-Wicke, which was Mrs Stump's maiden name) had ever had, neatly snipped out and saved.

It may not sound much to you, writing a letter, but this was a big deal for Fizz.

106

And he couldn't not shake Cedric's out-stretched hand. Fizz just knew the bully would make life unbearable if he backed out now. He'd go on and on about it to all the other kids, to everyone he met, and they all thought Cedric was so cool.

The sun was glinting off Cedric's leather jacket. He nibbled another nail, squinted at Fizz.

'So?' he said, his hand outstretched.

'Okay,' Fizz said, shaking it. 'But it won't be me writing the letter,' he added, trying to sound certain. 'You'll be the one doing the writing, saying how great *I* am.'

He felt sick.

Cedric chuckled a cold little laugh and turned to go away. Then he turned back to look at Fizz.

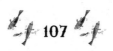

'Oh, do you know what, *Lump*? That wasn't even what I came to talk to you about. I only came to tell you that you and your stupid squidge-nosed girlfriend had better watch out. I'll break every one of her vases and rearrange her flowers if she so much as comes near me again. That was all I wanted to say. You'd both better watch out.'

'She's not my –' Fizz began, but Cedric spat another crescent of fingernail at the ground, spun on his fancy heel and strode off.

'I'm sorry I missed your friend,' Apology said, coming over. 'He looked very "cool". And I'm sorry the mice aren't being very cooperative today. I don't think it's going to work out, Fizzlebert, my boy. I'm so sorry but I don't think you're cut out for mouse-taming. You've either got it or you don't. I'm sorry.'

At dinner that evening the boys reconvened and spotted Dr Surprise queuing for his food. They picked their trays up and joined the queue just behind him.

'Did you talk to the farmer?' Fizz asked.

The Doctor jumped.

'Oh, Fizzlebert,' he said, straightening his top hat and fixing his monocle back in place. 'I didn't see you there.'

'Sorry, Doctor,' Fizz apologised (spending an hour with Cheesemutter had left its mark).

'As it happens I did manage to find a minute with Mr Gomez.'

'And . . . ?'

'I'm sorry to say, Wystan, dear boy, that Mr and Mrs X aren't your parents. They arrived several years ago from France. Mr Gomez said, they don't have amnesia, they're just foreign, that's why they seem a bit odd. See, it's all perfectly clear. I'm sorry, Wystan.'

'But that can't be true,' Wystan said loudly, banging his tray on the serving table. 'They're

me mum and dad. I know it. I'm sure of it.
I knew they weren't dead.'

'Ah, Hope,' said the Doctor, with a capital H. He lifted his hat and slipped a stick of celery underneath it. 'It is the only thing that keeps the world going. That and Hypnotism.'

'Hmph,' said Wystan, flapping his beard.

'Oh, but there was one good thing,' Dr Surprise said, his monocle twinkling with delight, as he looked both ways to make sure no one but the boys was listening. 'The lovely farmer told me, in strictest confidence mind you, that Flopples and I had impressed him very much with the act. Although the actual line-up won't be announced until Saturday, he hinted that there may well be a certain rabbit and her doctor on the bill.' He looked around again, straightened his moustache and tapped

the side of his nose with a lettuce leaf. 'Hush-hush,' he said. 'Not a word, yes?'

The boys nodded and the Doctor went and sat with the Ringmaster.

Wystan and Fizz went and sat by themselves at a different table.

'Well, that worked out *great,* Fizz. Thanks for nothing,' Wystan muttered, sarcastically.

'I'm sorry,' Fizz said. 'But it might've worked. It was worth trying. Mr Gomez was more likely to listen to Dr Surprise than us, wasn't he?'

'So, now what?'

'I don't believe Gomez's story. Do you?'

'Of course not.'

'Madame Plume de Matant showed me a picture of some French people in a book once and they didn't look like that.'

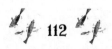

'So what do we do?'

'I suppose we're just going to have to try to find them and jog their memories ourselves. It's no use getting anyone else involved. If Dr Surprise believes Gomez, then so will the rest of the adults. You know what they're like. They never believe us right until the end.'

Wystan tugged his beard in agreement.

'But there must be loads of ways to get people to remember, if we can get to them. It's forever happening in books.' Fizz tried to think of some of the ways people got their memories back in some of the things he'd read over the years. 'I think we could give them a shock, or a bang on the head, or show them lots of pictures, or just talk to them, maybe let them stroke your beard, or sing them a song that they used to sing to you, or you

could make them little cakes that they used to love . . . there are all sorts of ways to reawaken memories. Until we've tried them all there's no giving up, okay?'

It was good to have something to concentrate on. A plan to come up with. It stopped him thinking about his still not having an act, or about Cedric's threats.

'I suppose,' Wystan said, agreeing grumpily with Fizz's list.

'Brilliant,' said Fizz. 'After dinner, get some dark clothes, your photograph, and be ready for a trip to the farmhouse.'

Again, Wystan had no choice but to agree. When Fizz was in this sort of mood nothing you said would get in his way. And Fizz was determined to be in this mood because the more he thought about Wystan's problem

the less his brain dwelt on his own dreadful dilemma.

Distraction, as the old saying that I just made up has it, *is as good as a cure.*

CHAPTER SIX

In which a farmhouse is entered
and in which a farmer is upset

'Fizzlebert Stump, hang on!' Alice said,
getting in Fizz's way.

Fizz and Wystan were creeping along the
hedgerow that divided their circus's field
from the next field along (which contained
the *Franklin, Franklin, Franklin & Daughter*'s
circus's caravans). They were heading to the

116

area in the middle of the fields where Mr Gomez's farmhouse stood.

'Hi, Alice,' said Fizz. He looked at Wystan and shrugged a 'Girls, what can you do?' sort of shrug.

'Where you off to?' she asked.

Fizz wasn't sure if he should say. His plan went as far as going to the farmhouse and seeing if they could find Wystan's parents and avoid Mr Gomez. Exactly how they'd do that he didn't know. Whatever happened he had a sneaking suspicion they'd have to find a way inside the farmhouse. Without asking. And that was just the sort of thing some people saw as being *wrong*. He didn't want Alice to come tagging along if they were going to get in trouble.

'Find me mum and dad, again,' Wystan said, making Fizz's decision for him.

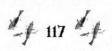

'Oh great!' Alice said, with what seemed to be genuine enthusiasm. 'Where are we going to look?'

'Up at the farmhouse. That's where we reckon they're going to be. That's where they live, you see.'

'Yeah, but we've got to watch out for Gomez,' Wystan added, pulling a beetle from his beard and flicking it into the hedgerow.

Fizz told Alice what Dr Surprise had said that Mr Gomez had told him about Mr and Mrs X's origins (Mr and Mrs X being the parentally moustachioed duo, obviously).

'You're in luck,' she said. 'He's having dinner with our Ringmaster. That's where my mum and dad are. Schmoozing with the farmer, hoping a good feed will make him like their acts more.'

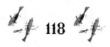

'Brilliant,' Fizz said. 'But we'd best get on, in and out before he finishes. Come on.'

And so they scuttled along by the hedge, whistling inconspicuously and trying to look casual.

I don't want you to think it was just Alice Crudge's Ringmaster that Mr Gomez was having dinner with. That would have been unfair. It was his habit, each year, to have a big dinner with each of the Ringmasters, all six, but not all on the same night because although he was a very large, round, corpulent (you could even say fat, after all he wouldn't be able to chase you very fast or very far if you did) man, he didn't want to look greedy.

Usually the Ringmasters would tell their Cooks to make the finest, biggest, most

luxurious slap-up feast they could find in their circus chef's cookbook, and Mr Gomez rather liked it when that happened. But sometimes a Ringmaster who had done a bit of extra homework, and found out that Mr Gomez farmed those odd-shaped vegetables that neither you nor I nor the farmer himself knew the name of, would get their Cooks to do *something special*. They would roast or they would boil or they would simmer or fricassee or mash or stuff or toast one of Mr Gomez's vegetables, thinking that he would appreciate the thought.

Unfortunately for them Mr Gomez *hated* the vegetables in question. He spent eleven months of the year looking forward to the day the circuses would arrive and trying his hardest to ignore the vegetables that provided

his livelihood. Like most people he thought they tasted bland, smelt weird and made an unpleasant noise when chewed. The last thing he wanted was to be reminded of them by a Ringmaster. That wasn't what Ringmasters were for, they were for serving up funny, exciting, unusual, magical, wonderful acts, shows and events. Not vegetables.

He had never been happier than on the day the hot air balloon had crashed into his farmhouse. (He wasn't happy right away, of course, because not only had a hot air balloon crashed into his farmhouse, but it was also raining. But when he'd realised exactly what it was that the balloon had delivered to him, the sun began to shine (metaphorically that is, since it rained for the rest of the morning and well into the afternoon).)

He had run downstairs in his pyjamas and out into the yard to see what damage had been done. It had soon become clear that the balloon's basket had bounced off the farmhouse without breaking so much as a window and had come to a stop in an old set of stables. The stables hadn't been used since Mr Gomez's father's day, when they had a couple of horses to pull the plough, but since he had bought a tractor thirty-one years ago all that lived in the stables were mice (not dogs).

Searching through the stable he had found two people spilt out of the basket on to the floor. They had had flying hats and goggles and moustaches and amnesia. (Alice had been right.) They had had no idea where they were or who they were. When Mr Gomez had asked them their names they had asked him what names were. When he had asked them what they did, they had asked him what did he mean?

Mr Gomez didn't become a rotten example of a human being right away. Not *right* away. His first thought had been to call a doctor, to get these people taken off his hands. After all, who would want a couple of injured people clogging up their farmhouse with broken legs and bandages and balloon-smell? But it had soon become clear that there were no broken limbs, just some bruises, bumps and lumps.

The three of them had sat at his kitchen table that lunchtime, sharing a pot of tea, and listening to the rain when he'd asked three questions that would change his life.

'Do either of you know anything about farming? About vegetables? Do you know what this is called?' (He'd put one of his odd-shaped vegetables on the table.)

'No. No. No,' his ballooning guests had said.

'Smashing,' Mr Gomez had said, rubbing his hands together. He tried three more

questions. 'Do either of you have somewhere better to be? Do you have anyone waiting for you out there beyond the storm? Is anyone going to be looking for you?'

'No. No. No,' they'd said (although that hadn't really meant anything, since they had amnesia and whether someone is looking for you or not doesn't change whether you believe, remember or hope they are looking for you or not).

And in fact the police *had* looked for their balloon, for weeks and weeks, but the storm had been so fierce and had blown them so far off course that they'd never thought to search Mr Gomez's farm.

And so, for years now, Mr Gomez had sat in the farmhouse eating aubergines and cucumbers and potatoes and broccoli

and carrots and lots of other things he knew the name of and liked the taste of, while his two house guests, knowing no better, remembering nothing else, and trusting the only person they thought they knew, went out every day and worked his fields. Mr X, as Mr Gomez had named the man with the moustache, enjoyed driving the tractor and Mrs X, as Mr Gomez had named the woman with the moustache, enjoyed packing the odd-shaped vegetables into boxes to be sent to the supermarkets. Neither of them much enjoyed the sowing and reaping and weeding and watering and fertilizing and so on, but they didn't have anywhere else to be and didn't know any better.

*

So now you know the truth of what's going on, we should go back to Fizz and the others as they sneak through the farmyard, past the barn where the hot air balloon is still packed away and past the stable where Wystan's parents first crash-landed.

Fizzlebert Stump had once broken into an aquarium and had once searched a caravan while its owners were away and he'd once escaped from a house like a (horribly untidy) prison. He wondered if any of those experiences would come in handy for finding their way into the farmhouse.

They peered over the edge of an old stone horse trough and looked at the building. It was a fairly large building with half a dozen bedrooms, most of which were unoccupied, Mr Gomez being the last of his line. It would take them a while to search it. They might have to split up. But before any of that they needed to get in.

'We could see if they've left a window open somewhere, maybe upstairs. I think I saw a ladder over there.' (Fizz pointed into the open-fronted stable they'd just crept past.) 'Or we could throw some stones at the roof and then when they come out to see what the noise is we could sneak in. Or . . . Alice?'

'Yes?'

'How strong are you?'

'Pretty.'

'Yes, I know, but how strong are you?'

(It was only after Fizz said the words that he realised that he'd misunderstood her first answer. He hoped no one noticed. He didn't want her thinking he was odd.)

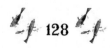

'Very, I think,' she said, using a more help-ful word.

'Could you push the door in? I mean even if it's locked?'

'I expect so. I once lifted the caravan when one of Dad's plates rolled underneath it. He didn't half get in a tizz about it. He doesn't approve. It's unladylike, he says. That's cob-blers, I say.'

'Flower Arranging,' muttered Wystan, beardily.

'Yes,' she said, turning away. 'It's embar-rassing. It's not an act, is it? Who wants to see live flower arranging? Even when we send the finished arrangement through a fiery hoop it's not exactly edge of your seat stuff. "Oh, look! Her gladioli's been singed." That's about as exciting as it gets.'

'Well, maybe you could do it on horseback or something,' Fizz said, trying to lighten the mood of the moment.

'Our horses have hay fever,' Alice said.

'That's ironic,' Fizz said. When no one laughed he went on, 'Because horses eat hay.'

No one laughed again.

'What I really want to do,' she went on, 'is lift things up. I mean, that's a *real* act, isn't it? Big things! Huge things! That's a challenge, that's a spectacle, *that's* a proper circus act. But Dad says it's not interesting enough. He says there are hundreds of Strongmen and Strongwomen out there. Flower Arranging, he says, will get us noticed, make us stand out, and that's what he wants. If we got a write-up in the Newsletter, some other circus might offer us a contract. It's pretty rubbish being with *Neil Coward's Cicrus*. We all know what people say about it — that it's where acts end up when they've run out of steam. Well, I'm young, I'm fresh, I've got a chance to escape. Anyway, that's what Dad says. I just wish he'd let me lift something up.'

'My dad's a Strongman,' Fizz said, not exactly changing the subject, but distracting it from the quite glum lecture about the *Cicrus*.

'I know,' Alice said, perking up. 'I've got a poster of him on my bedroom wall. I think he's brilliant. I've memorised the list of all the things he lifted last year. It was in the BBC Newsletter New Year Edition. He's my hero.'

That was weird, Fizz thought. He liked his dad, for sure. He thought his dad's act was good, but . . . it wasn't *so* good that a girl like Alice should have memorised the list of things he picked up. Was it? Did Fizz feel jealous? Was that what this feeling was? Would he have preferred it if she'd memorised the list of things he'd put his head in instead? (To be fair she probably *had* memorised that list because it contained one thing, a very toothy and impressive thing to be sure, but still, just one.)

'Fizz,' Wystan said, either ruining or saving the moment. 'Look, there's a light on in the kitchen, I think they're having their dinner. Why don't we go knock on the back door?'

'Oh, alright then,' Fizz said. 'After you.'

'Hello?' said the moustachioed man called Mr X who was almost certainly Wystan's father.

'Hi, can we come in?' Wystan asked.

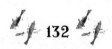

'Well, we were just having our dinner.'

'It's important,' Fizz said over Wystan's shoulder.

'Who is it, Mr X?' called a lady's voice from inside.

'Some short people,' Mr X replied. 'They want to come in.'

'Will they be long?'

'No, they're quite short.'

'Your potatoes are getting cold.'

'I've got potatoes?' he said, turning to look back into the kitchen.

'Quick!' Fizz said, pushing Wystan through the doorway.

Alice and Fizz followed and when Mr X turned round to look back into the farmyard to continue his conversation he was faced with a cool evening, empty of children and

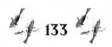

beginning to cloud over. The wind was getting up in the east and it looked like it might rain soon.

'Wind's up. Fifteen, maybe seventeen knots, north-north-east,' he said, shutting the back door.

'What's that?' Mrs X said.

'What's what?'

As Mr X turned he jumped in surprise (only a little, he was a full-grown man with an impressive moustache after all; but still, there was a noticeable movement).

'Who are you?' he said to the kitchenful of children.

'They just appeared, dear,' Mrs X said. 'Short people all over the place. I wondered if they were with you.'

'I don't think so,' he replied.

'We've come to talk to you,' Fizz said. 'We want to ask you some questions.'

'Oh, questions,' Mrs X said. 'Are you from the newspaper?'

Before Fizz could say, 'No,' Alice said, 'Yes.' She went on, 'We're investigating a story about some missing balloonists.'

'What are they?'

'You know,' said Mr X. 'We saw one this afternoon. Twisting. Turning. Folding. He made a . . . Oh, what was it?'

'A snake?' asked Mrs X.

'No. A worm,' said Mr X.

'I think that's the wrong sort of balloonist,' Alice said. 'The ones we're looking for flew balloons. Hot air balloons.'

'In the sky?' said Mrs X, looking at the ceiling as if it weren't there.

'Yes,' said Fizz. 'And they got lost. We think they must've landed here. Maybe they crashed.'

'Oh, I don't think so,' said Mr X. 'We'd've noticed something like that. What colour did you say the balloon was?'

'I don't know. I don't know what colour the balloon was, but –'

Wystan was standing behind the other two. Fizz had made this sound like it would be easy, as if they'd just walk in and show them the photo and watch their eyes de-cloud, see the mist lift and hear them say, 'Welcome back, son'. But it wasn't that easy. He was holding the photo in its frame under his jacket. It felt hard and real, but showing it off, that seemed the opposite – it seemed unreal. In short, it was *scary*. What if it didn't work? What if they got angry? What if he had it wrong? What if it was all just an act? What if they knew full well who he was, but didn't want a freak like him for a son?

'Look at this,' he said, interrupting Fizz and surprising himself.

'What is it?' asked Mrs X.

'It's a short man with a beard, dear,' said Mr X.

'No, I wasn't talking to you, silly. I was talking *to* the short man with the beard.'

'I'm not a man,' Wystan said.

'Sorry,' Mrs X corrected herself. 'I was talking to the short *woman* with the beard.'

'I'm not a woman, either,' Wystan said, stamping his feet.

'Oh, I know this one,' Mr X said, stroking his moustache. 'A short *hallucination* with a beard.'

'No,' said Wystan. 'I'm not a hallucination, I'm real and I'm a boy. Just a boy.'

'That explains a lot,' Mr X said, not explaining what he thought it explained.

'My name's Wystan,' Wystan said, not beating about the bush any more. 'And I reckon you're me mum and dad. Look at this photo.'

He handed the picture frame over to Mrs X, who had stood up from her place at the table.

'What a handsome couple,' she said.

'Oh yes,' said Mr X, looking over her shoulder.

'Is that you in the middle?' she asked, pointing at the bearded baby in the photo.

'Yes,' said Wystan. 'And that's you either side of me. You're me mum and dad.'

Mr X looked at Mrs X and shook his head.

'I'm sorry, lad,' he said. 'But I think you've mistaken us for someone else.'

'That can't be us there,' Mrs X said, handing the photo back. 'We've never been in a photograph. We're from France, you see.'

'You're not from France,' Wystan said. 'You're from Basingstoke. Your names are Wilfred and Hester Humphreys. You're famous balloonists who flew a hot air balloon called the *Golden Goose*, you are explorers of places people have already been to, you're aerial musicians, fashion models and disc jockeys, *and* you're me mum and dad.'

He stamped his foot again in frustration.

'Don't you mean Barboozul?' asked Fizz quietly, confused.

'That's a stage name Lord and Lady Barboozul came up with, Fizz,' Wystan said. 'No one has such silly names in real life.'

'Is Basingstoke in France?' asked Mrs X.

'No,' said Wystan.

'Well, I don't think we come from there, then.'

'Where do you come from?' asked Alice.

'Oh, France. Somewhere. Apparently.'

'Apparently?'

'Yes, that's what the nice man says. I forget myself.'

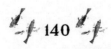

'Yes, it's all a bit of blur, yesterday.'

'Yesterday?'

'Yes, when we arrived.'

'From France?'

'Apparently.'

Fizz didn't know what to do. It seemed the conversation was going round and round in circles. There hadn't been a glimmer of recognition from the moustachioed pair. Not the faintest sign of a spark when they saw the picture or when Wystan told them their real names.

Then someone began singing. Singing in a furry falsetto.

'Up in the air, the balloon rocks away,
the baby sleeps well, until break of day.
The winds blow us up and blow us along,
the baby sleeps well, all the night long.'

'That's a nice tune,' Mrs X said, humming it to herself.

'It's what you used to sing,' Wystan said, his beard quivering. 'It was the lullaby you used to sing me.'

Mrs X looked blank.

Suddenly the door burst open and a huge round shape lumbered into the kitchen shouting, 'What's going on here!?'

Fizz stuttered something and Alice coughed and Wystan hid in his beard.

It was Mr Gomez, squeezing through the doorway. He pulled his dark glasses off and hung them in his shirt pocket.

'These short people,' Mrs X said, indicating the trio, 'have come to sing us some songs. About balloons.'

'Balloons?' said Mr Gomez suspiciously.

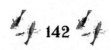

'Forget the balloons,' said Fizz, drawing himself up to his full height and feeling the power of the moment burn through him. 'We're here because a boy ought to have parents. If there's *any* chance of finding them, of being with them, a boy should grab it with both hands.'

'Too true,' said Mr Gomez. 'Perhaps we should go find *your* parents. I open my fields up to the circuses, but this farmhouse is my *home*. This is mine, little man. This is where I come of an evening and put my feet up after a long day. I can't just let anyone come barging in here, especially when I'm not home.'

'But we didn't come to see *you*,' said Wystan, pointing at the large farmer with the corner of the picture frame (he pointed with the rest of the picture frame too, but the corner went furthest). 'We came to see me mum and dad.'

'Your . . . ? Oh! There *was* some bloke round here earlier asking about this, wasn't there? Professor Present or something.'

'Dr Surprise,' corrected Fizz.

'Yeah, well I told him what I'll tell you. My friends here don't speak much English. Whatever you've said to them, they've not understood because they're not from round

here. They're French, over here on a holiday. Ain't that right?'

He looked at Mr X.

'Oh yes,' he responded. 'That's what you say.'

'They're nothing to do with *you*.' He noticed the picture Wystan was waving and snatched it from his hand. 'What's this?'

'It's the only picture I've got of me and me mum and dad,' Wystan said.

'He's called Winston,' Mrs X said, looking over Mr Gomez's fat shoulder. 'The little lad there. The bearded chap said so.'

'Not *Winston*,' Wystan corrected, '*Wystan*.'

'I know you,' said Mr Gomez suddenly, peering closer and wheezing courgette breath into Wystan's face. 'You're the Bearded Boy. Something Barboozul. Now I recognise you.

You're on the schedule tomorrow morning aren't you?'

'Yes, me and Fish.'

'Well, boy,' Mr Gomez said with an ugly sneer. 'You're *not*.'

'Not what?'

'Not on the schedule.'

'What?'

Mr Gomez waved Wystan's photo round as he spoke, using it to illustrate his points.

'Firstly, *your* sea lion attacked some clowns. A fish in the custard. Secondly, *your* sea lion attacked Raymond Piles as he was balancing an occasional table on top of a snooker cue on top of a champagne bottle on top of his chin. Turned out there was a fish in the drawer. His confidence was shattered, as was his snooker cue, and his champagne bottle, and his occasional table. Thirdly, when Madame Long-Plunge jumped off her high platform to swan dive into a small paddling pool forty feet below (an act, might I add, that I adore) her fall was broken abruptly by a sea lion. *Your* sea lion. There were fish in the pool she hadn't known about. Fourthly –'

'But it's not Fish's fault, he just goes where his nose takes him,' Fizz said.

'Was the lady alright?' Alice asked.

'I wouldn't say she was exactly happy about it,' Mr Gomez snapped.

'But, how did the fish get there? In the pool and in the custard and in the drawer?' Fizz asked. 'Someone must've –'

'Dunno, and it's not important. The problem's not the fish, it's the sea lion. I've had words with your Ringmaster. He's locking it up for the rest of the week. I can't have him running around ruining any more shows. So that means that you, my bearded wonder, are out of an act. So sorry.' (He didn't sound sorry.)

Wystan's beard quivered.

'Can I have my picture back?'

'Oh, as for this?' Gomez looked at the photo. 'It's nothing. You come in here accusing perfectly innocent French people of being your long-lost parents. What do you expect? They look nothing like this pair here. The moustaches are different. The clothes are different. You're barking up the wrong tree. Answer me this, were your mum and dad French?'

'No.'

He shoved Wystan's photo into the boy's hands.

'Then, case closed. Now, get out of here before I kick you out.' He turned back to his moustachioed house-guests-cum-farm-labourers. 'I'm so sorry you had to be faced with this, this . . . nonsense. It must be upsetting to you. I'm so sorry, but they're kids.' He shrugged. 'What can you do?'

But Mr and Mrs X had already sat back down at the table and were just putting their cutlery together on their now empty plates.

'Sorry?' Mr X said. 'Oh, visitors! How interesting.'

Fizz and his friends were dejected. Mr Gomez hadn't exactly been friendly. The meeting hadn't exactly gone as planned. And Wystan

had exactly lost his chance to perform in the Circus of Circuses show, although that bothered him much less than having been so close to his mum and dad while they were so far away from him. But still, poor Fish getting locked up.

Tomorrow is another day, Fizz thought, climbing into bed later that night, although it looked like being a miserable one for him and his friends.

CHAPTER SEVEN

In which a boy lifts things
up above his head and in
which revenge is plotted

Fizz spent an uneasy night in his fold-down-dining-room-table-cum-bed (this wasn't a punishment, just a sign that the Stumps' caravan wasn't very big). He didn't get a lot of sleep, lying there thinking about all the things that had happened and worrying and wondering what might happen next. How to solve Wystan's problem, how to solve his own.

He also lay awake thinking, if he was having this much trouble sleeping, what must poor Wystan be going through?

But eventually he did sleep, because the next thing he knew he was being woken up.

'Come on, Fizz. Wakey wakey,' his dad was saying, lifting him up with one hand and folding his bed back into the wall with the other.

'Okay,' Fizz said, blearily. 'Okay.'

As they had breakfast, a few minutes later, he asked his dad a question.

'Dad?' he said. 'You know I've been looking for a new act? For something to do?'

'Yes, son,' his dad said. 'Course I do. I thought you'd end up helping Wystan out with the acrobatics.' (Fizz had, very occasionally,

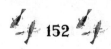

joined in with Wystan and Fish's tumbling and balancing act.) 'But I hear Fish is in the doghouse.'

'The doghouse?'

'Well, *lionhouse*. Fox-Dingle's been told to keep him locked up in one of his cages, just while the trials are on. He's been doing mischief, apparently.'

'Yeah, we heard that,' Fizz said gloomily. 'I was wondering, Dad, if I might help you, in your act?'

'Help *me*?'

'Yeah, you know. Lifting things up or just pointing at things for you. I reckon I could be useful.'

'I don't know, Fizz,' his dad said, stroking his little moustache. 'It's not as easy as it looks. You're only a lad –'

'I know, but I'm pretty strong,' Fizz said. 'Remember when I was trapped in that trunk and I heaved all the stuff off the top? That took muscles.' (He was referring to something that happened in *Fizzlebert Stump and the Bearded Boy*, just in case you didn't know.) 'And what about the time Bongo Bongoton dropped that weight on his foot and couldn't move? He was trapped there for hours before I came along and lifted it up for him. No one else had been able to.'

'But, Fizz, he's a mime and it was an imaginary weight.'

'Okay, not the best example,' Fizz said. 'Forget that one, but the trunk was real and I carried all those books back to the library for Dr Surprise the other week. He reads dead heavy books.'

Mr Stump twirled his moustache and made a thoughtful face. '*Stump & Son*,' he said as if testing the words.

'That sounds good, doesn't it?' Fizz asked, eagerly.

This was one of the things he'd thought during the night. He'd been given the idea by something Alice had mentioned. It definitely wasn't that he wanted to impress her by becoming a Strongman, by doing an act with his dad (whose poster she had up on her bedroom wall). No, it wasn't that at all. Definitely not. No. If you'd suggested that that was what it was, Fizz would have protested, told you to stop being silly, blushed, fiddled with his buttons and changed the subject. He didn't know exactly why he thought it would be a good idea, but all of a sudden he did.

And if Alice just happened to think it was cool, then that was up to her.

'I tell you what, Fizz,' his dad said, having stroked his chin (which is how a Strongman makes decisions). 'We'll try some stuff out this morning. See how it goes. I've got to do the act for Mr Gomez tomorrow. I'm practically the last act he's going to see. So we've got until then. If it doesn't work out, I'll do the normal act. Yes? But if we can fit you in, then we'll do it? That sound okay?'

'Yeah,' said Fizz, enthusiastically.

(In case anyone was wondering why this was a quite straightforward breakfast (they were eating a custard kedgeree Fizz's mum had made the night before) with no clown antics, honking, hiding or silliness the answer is easy: *Mrs Stump wasn't there.*

Why weren't Fizz and Mr Stump worried? Why weren't they searching for her? Why did they not even seem to notice her absence?

Well, that answer's easy too: she left before the two men sat down for their breakfast to go and rehearse with the rest of the clowns. They were being seen by Gomez that afternoon and were busy with final adjustments and preparations. (Checking custard for foreign objects, such as Danish fish.)

She had said goodbye perfectly sensibly ten minutes ago but I thought it was too boring a scene to put into the book, so I left it out.)

So, that morning Fizz and his dad practised.

They began with small things. Mr Stump handed Fizz a tin of custard (not a normal-size tin with one or two portions in, like you

or I might eat with a spoon all by ourselves, but a big catering-sized tin that can feed a whole roomful of hungry people, like you or I might eat by ourselves when no one else is watching).

Fizz took hold of the can, wobbled, slipped and dropped it on his foot.

'Oh golly,' he said in pain. 'That hurt.'

'The thing about a Strongman rather than a clown, Fizz,' his dad explained, 'is that we don't just hold things for a second, then drop them. We hold them up and keep them up. That's what an audience really wants to see.'

'I know that,' Fizz said, stretching his toes inside his shoe. Nothing was broken. 'I just didn't get the grip right. It slipped.'

He squatted down and wrapped his fingers around the can.

He took a deep breath and lifted and lifted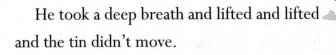
and the tin didn't move.

'What's in here?' he asked.

'Just custard, Fizz,' his dad said. 'Your mum
lifts it every day.'

'Not a tin this big,' Fizz complained. 'She
has it in a bucket.'

'Do you know what?' his dad said. 'I'm going to let you into a secret. I'm not very good at lifting things. Not really. Not straight away. I have to *think* myself strong. Oh, sure I've got muscles the size of your head, but they're no good if I'm not *thinking* right.'

'How do you do that?'

'You remember when you were in the Barboozuls' trunk?'

'Of course.'

'It was dark. You were in trouble. We were all in trouble. You were scared.'

'I wasn't *that* scared,' Fizz clarified.

'You were scared enough that your *Inner Strongman* heard you and when push came to pull, it pushed with you.'

'My *Inner Strongman*?' Fizz said, dubiously.

'Yep. You need to find what's important to you, Fizz, find what makes you *want* to lift the weight. Me, I think about your mum. Oh, Fizz, I love that clown so much. When I first met her I could barely lift the front end of a blindfolded baby bison. But I so wanted to impress her. I wanted to make her proud. I still do. When I find something's getting heavy, getting hard to lift, I just think about her standing behind me, her bow tie spinning and her horn sighing with love. Oh!'

'Dad,' Fizz said, embarrassed and appalled at what he was hearing. 'Shut up.'

'In my mind's eye,' his dad went on, 'when I'm lifting something *really* heavy, I see your mum coming over and kissing me. It makes me laugh as her nose tickles my moustache, but –'

'La-la-la-la,' Fizz sang, covering his ears.

His dad stopped talking and waved the hands away.

'Fizz,' he said. 'If you don't pick that tin up, I'll tell you more about how much I love your mum.'

Fizz bent down and, with one hand, tucked the tin of custard under his arm, balanced it on his knee, got his other hand round it and lifted it above his head. His muscles bulged under his coat and he could feel his heart racing in his chest, but he was doing it, it was working!

'Just so long as you're quiet, Dad,' he said.

Fizz had discovered one of the keys to unlocking his Inner Strongman: the desperate desire to avoid embarrassment. What he would never tell his dad (or anyone, not

even you (not even me)) was that at the same time, he was sort of, maybe, imagining Alice Crudge watching and being impressed. But not really, no. It was definitely just the desire to make his dad shut up.

After experimenting with several tins of custard Fizz got some of his dad's dumbbells out of the caravan (it rose a little when they were removed).

He lifted one of them above his head and twirled it like a drum majorette.

'Careful, Fizz,' his dad said. 'You could have someone's eye out with that.'

It was a silly thing to say, since the dumbbell had a round metal sphere at either end, completely useless for poking things out. But *very* good for knocking people out. (His dad was right to suggest safety, but wrong in his choice of words. After all, he was a strongman, not William Shakespeare.)

(It was just at this moment that Alexander Fakespeer wandered past in the background, saying, 'A horse! A horse! My kingdom for a horse.' (Fortunately he was nowhere nearby Miss Tremble's caravan, because as much as she loved her horses, she might've swapped one of them for a whole kingdom. You never know.))

Fizz lifted a second dumbbell in his other hand and began twirling the pair of them.

This was going well, he thought.

He could feel his muscles working. They were strong. They were meaty. They were manly. He had occasionally felt something of his dad's blood course in his veins, but in his

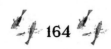

previous act, with the lion, he'd never got to show it off. He might've been able to pick Charles up, if he'd only tried. Imagine what sort of act that would have been: The Boy Who Picks a Lion Up and Lowers Its Mouth Around His Own Head. Gosh! Golly! If only he'd thought of it back then.

But, thinking all this, he lost concentration for a second. He fumbled a spin and the twirling dumbbells clanged into each other, stopped twirling abruptly, jarred his wrist, wobbled themselves and fell in a clattering, thudding pair of deep thuds into the earth either side of him.

'Less twirling, Fizz,' his dad said. 'Strongmen don't do a lot of twirling normally. Lifting it up's usually good enough.'

He looked around as if to make sure no one was watching and said, 'I think it's time for a tea break, don't you?'

'I suppose,' said Fizz, feeling a little less confident.

'Here, catch this,' his dad said, tossing him a whole cake.

It looked like a Victoria sponge or something (Fizz wasn't an expert, although he was

a fan): two layers of pale cake with jam gluing them together in the middle.

He caught the cake easily and looked around for somewhere to put it down.

His father was unfolding a little picnic table.

'There you go,' he said.

He put a plate, just big enough for the cake, on top.

Fizz gently put the cake on to the plate and stood back.

There was a creak of wood, a crack of porcelain, and then the table collapsed. The plate and the cake fell straight through it to the ground.

'Dad!' Fizz shouted. 'That's not –'

'Yep,' his dad confirmed. 'That's a Madame Plume de Matant special. I told her it was your birthday.'

Madame Plume de Matant was the circus's fortune teller. She usually set up in a little booth by the entrance to the Big Top and audience members would pop in and cross her palm with money before the show to find out what their futures held. She was also the woman who was supposed to be teaching Fizzlebert French, which was why he hadn't been able to try any French out on Mr and Mrs X. In addition to being a faux French teacher and a fraudulent (yet entertaining) fortune teller, she was also the worst, most self-deluded home baker in the entire circus.

Her cakes were legendary.

They broke tables, teeth and cutlery.

And his dad had got him one for his birthday (even though it wasn't his birthday for

another seven months, two weeks and six days). That was a bit weird.

'I thought at this point we'd invite someone from the audience to try picking it up,' his dad said.

Percy Late (of *Percy Late and his Spinning Plate* fame) happened to be chasing one of his runaway plates nearby.

'Hey, Percy,' Mr Stump shouted. 'Come over here a moment.'

Percy, having captured the errant piece of crockery, wandered over to see what all the fuss was.

'Here, Percy,' Mr Stump said. 'We've dropped a cake. Could you pick it up for us?'

Percy looked at Mr Stump, then he looked at Fizz and he said, 'What's going on here? Two fine strong lads like you pair and you

can't pick up a little sponge cake like that?
There's something fishy going on here, isn't
there?'

Nevertheless, despite his suspicions, Percy
was a good chap and bent down to lift the
cake.

At first he tried using one hand but the
thing wouldn't budge. Then he got his other
hand on it, under it and tried tugging. It still
wasn't going anywhere.

'Is it glued?' he asked.

'No, no glue,' Fizz said.

'Let me get a better position,' Percy mumbled, moving round so his feet were either
side of the cake and his fingers were wriggling right underneath. 'Heave!'

The only thing that moved was a bead of
sweat on Percy's forehead.

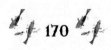

'Hang on,' he said, straightening up again. 'Is that one of . . .'

'It's just a *cake*, Percy,' Mr Stump said.

Percy looked at him. It was a quizzical look, verging on the suspicious.

'Who made it?' he asked carefully.

'I don't know,' Mr Stump said, acting all innocent-like. 'Your plates, Percy, who makes those?'

Percy lifted the plate from the grass where he'd put it and showed the Stumps the underside.

'That's easy to find out. Look, it says there: *Llanfairpwllgwyngyllgogerychwyrndrobw llllantysiliogogogoch Pots and Pans Ltd.*'

'See that, Fizz?' his dad asked. 'To find the maker of a thing, you have to look on the underneath.'

Fizz took the cue and heaved the cake up with one hand. It was heavy but he could do it, and do it with a smile as if he were in the ring (never show the strain, not for a cake). He turned it over and there was no writing on the bottom at all. Not a single word.

'How did you . . . ?' stumbled Percy Late, pointing at Fizz. 'Oh!' he said, 'are you doing a double act now?'

'Maybe, maybe,' Fizz's dad said. 'We'll see.'

Some time later Wystan wandered over.

He looked glum (or as glum as someone with a big beard can look).

'How's it going?' asked Fizz, putting a motorbike down. (I say 'motorbike' but it was really just a little motorized scooter thing (not even half as heavy as a full-grown

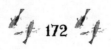

sea lion), but still it was something I think would impress an audience. I mean, I probably couldn't pick one up, so it impresses me.)

All this lifting things up, all this work, had quite taken Fizz's mind off his bearded pal's problems. For a moment he'd forgotten why Wystan was looking so melancholy. (By which I don't mean looking like the famous hybrid fruit/vegetable, which is spelt quite differently: meloncauli (not to be confused with the hybrid dog/vegetable, the meloncollie). Mr Gomez didn't grow either of those. You can tell because I know their names. And because I just made them up.)

The bearded boy blew a bearded raspberry by way of answer to Fizz's question. (And,

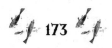

before you ask, Gomez didn't grow bearded raspberries either: they're a *fruit* and the things he grew were vegetables.)

'Oh, sorry,' Fizz said.

'It don't matter,' said Wystan. 'It's just all a bit –' He blew a second raspberry. 'Me and Fish were supposed to . . . you know, do the show and he's miserable. I've been sitting with him. He's in Charles's old cage. Everything's a bit miserable over there. Fox-Dingle's having trouble with Kate.' (The crocodile, not my editor.) 'She keeps eating his chair.' (Lion tamers traditionally use a chair and a whip to train their big cats. They hold the chair out with its legs facing the wild animal so that it can't jump at the trainer. This works for cats because they don't like to eat furniture (rip it, shred, it, bite it, yes, but only if it's

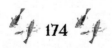

upholstered). Crocodiles, on the other hand, are clearly less choosey about what they eat.)

'He's not even sure *he'll* have an act to show off tomorrow either. And then that Cedric kid was hanging around.'

'Cedric?' Fizz asked with a shiver. (It wasn't that he was afraid, it was just that in the excitement of the act he'd almost forgotten about Greene's very existence. Sometimes just being reminded that something rotten still exists can be enough to give you a shiver up your spine.)

'Yeah. Leather jacket. Bites his nails. No beard. Thinks he's the big boss.'

'I know the one,' Fizz said.

'He kept bothering old Dingle-Dangle with questions.'

'Questions?'

'Yeah: "Here, mate, how do you make a lion like you?" and "Hey, Cap, how do you stop a lion dribbling?" and "Yo, Foxy, how do you find out a lion's name?" Things like that.'

'Oh,' said Fizz. He didn't know if he felt good about this or not. He didn't like the idea of Cedric talking to Captain Fox-Dingle, but he did like the thought that Cedric needed help with his lion. 'But he told me his Putting His Head in the Lion's Mouth act was brilliant. He said it was already perfect. But . . .'

'You should have seen the Captain's face,' Wystan said, smiling for the first time. 'It was a picture.'

'What did he say? Did he answer?'

'Oh yeah.' Wystan straightened himself up like Fox-Dingle and did his best impression of having a small toothbrush moustache.

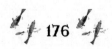

He stared at Fizz and snapped out a one-word answer exactly as the Captain would've.

'"Love"', he said.

Fizz laughed.

'Oh gosh,' he said. 'What did Cedric say to that?'

'Nothing. He just looked annoyed and left. But before he did he said, "Whatever," and threw Fish a fish.'

'A fish?'

'For Fish.'

'That's weird.'

'Just pulled it out his pocket and chucked it in the cage.'

'Did he say anything else?'

'Um, let me think.' Wystan pulled a notebook out of his beard and flipped the pages. 'I made a note,' he said. He found the right page, ran his finger down it and said, '"Loser."'

'He said that?'

'Yep.'

'It was him.'

'What was him?'

'The fish.'

'The sabotage?'

'Yep.'

'But why?'

'Being the big man means a lot to him,' Fizz said. 'He wants to win, and what better way of winning is there than having your circus win the most?'

'His circus?' Wystan said.

'Yeah, none of the acts that were ruined were from *A Ring & A Prayer*, were they? He's trying to take out the competition. Trying to get as many of his circus's acts into the Circus of Circuses show on Saturday.'

Wystan mumbled an insult into his beard. I didn't hear exactly what it was, but somewhere the other side of the farm Cedric's ears itched.

'Yep and did you know,' Fizz went on, 'his dad's the Ringmaster? I remember reading it in the BBC Newsletter.'

'Do you think his dad knows what Cedric's doing?'

'I don't know,' Fizz said. Even if he believed Ringmaster Greene was involved there was no one he could tell. His own Ringmaster would never accuse another Ringmaster of being dishonest. Mr Gomez, whose Circus of Circuses the whole Gathering was about, would never listen to Fizz and Wystan, not after last night.

There was nothing they could do.

'Fish is locked away, so the sabotage is over,' Fizz said.

'You mean the sabotage *worked*,' Wystan said. 'I don't care about the rest, but because of him I've got no act. But I don't even care about that. It's 'cause of him that Gomez was angry about *Fish* and angry with *me*. If he'd

not had the sea lion ruining everything all day then he'd've been in a better mood last night. He'd've listened to me properly when I told him about me mum and dad. If only Cedric Greene hadn't made poor Fish ruin everything.'

'I don't know about that,' Fizz said, trying to calm his friend down a bit.

Wystan's beard was prickling with pent-up rage. His eyes flared over the top of it. They were red, glistening with unfallen tears. Fizz had never seen him so agitated, so passionate, so angry.

'It's all Cedric's fault,' Wystan declared, waving a finger in the air. 'I've made a decision, Fizz. Two can play at that game. I'm going to get him back.'

'Um, okay,' said Fizz, not certain that revenge was the best plan. 'How?'

CHAPTER EIGHT

In which some clowns perform
brilliantly and in which some
flower arranging goes awry

That afternoon, while Wystan was off
plotting the finer points of his plan (or
so he said), Fizz made his way, with his dad,
to the Big Top, where his mother's troupe of
clowns were going to show off their show in
front of Mr Gomez and the two Xs. Theirs
wasn't the only act being observed this afternoon, the timetable Fizz had in his pocket also

listed 'Botanic Acts [1]' and 'Terpsichorean Acts (Canine) [3]'. (A quick word of explanation about how the timetable was laid out: first there's the category of the act ('Botanic' means 'to do with flowers', 'Terpsichorean' means 'to do with dance' and 'Canine' means 'to do with dogs' (not mice)) and then the numbers in square brackets tell you the number of different acts competing in that category. Therefore, after the clowns, there was one flower act and three sets of dancing dogs to watch.)

Fizz was excited for two reasons. Firstly, he'd almost, sort of, got an act together with his dad, which meant he'd be out there in the sawdust tomorrow afternoon, vying for a chance of being in the big show. This made him feel so much better that he practically felt

like a new boy (it had lifted a weight off his shoulders, lifting the weights with his hands). And secondly, and this one he was keeping secret, he had a suspicion that there was only one person doing a Botanic Act, and that was Alice. Although she gave the impression that Flower Arranging wasn't the greatest circus act of all time and although no one expected much from a *Neil Coward's Famous Cicrus* act, Fizz was willing to give it a try. He reckoned it might just be better than she made out.

Fizz and his dad watched the clowns be brilliant. Everything went to plan. Not a single act of sabotage intruded on the comedy gold that was pouring out of their trousers, buckets and flowers-in-buttonholes-that-squirted-water-when-least-expected. They fell over

their feet, they hit each other with ladders and planks, and their car fell to bits almost as soon as it drove into the ring. Clowns wept and custard flew and whitewash spilt. The Big Top filled with the noise of swannee whistles, honking horns and deep guffaws as Big Bert Boomer (*The Jolly Old Gloomer*) pointed at every mishap and boomed his big booming laugh like a joyous schadenfreude bittern (which is a brilliant similie of mine that might make more sense once you've looked it up in a dictionary or be friended a German ornithologist).

Mrs Stump, *The Fumbling Gloriosus*, lived up to her name. Fizz couldn't remember the last time he'd seen her be so clumsy. *The Amusing Graham Smith* (the least interestingly named clown in the circus, but he'd only been with them a few months and everyone said he was sure to find a more clownish name in time, when he'd got a bit more experience) handed Mrs Stump things for her to hold: a telescope, a teapot, a tiddlywink, a tortoise (stuffed), a Pterodactyl (model), a turban (cloth) and she dropped every one of them.

But she didn't just drop them, she *fumbled* them. And she didn't just *fumble* them, she fumbled them *gloriously*. For a moment it looked like she had a grip on whatever it was, but then it began to slip, but she got her hand underneath it, and then it wobbled the other way, and as she tried to keep a hold of whatever it was that was slowly escaping her clutches her face was a marvel to see. Oh! The surprise on it. Oh! The disappointment on it. Oh! The sadness, the shock . . . and then . . . Oh! The silly grin as she got a firm hold on, say, the teapot and held it above her head, triumphantly (like a slightly proud Strongman), only for the lid to fall out and hit her square on the bonce.

The surprise of which caused her to drop the teapot itself, which also bounced off her skull on the way down.

She was brilliant.

Had there been an audience there, other than the dozen circus folk scattered around and about in the Big Big Top, then the roars of laughter and applause would have been deafening.

But there wasn't an audience there and the smattering of clapping sounded tiny and pathetic in the huge, almost empty space.

Nevertheless Fizz noticed that Mr Gomez was smiling as he turned to Mr and Mrs X, to compare notes, or to get their opinions before they forgot what they'd just seen (or at least to make it look like he was including them), and they too had big grins under their curled moustaches.

As the last dribble of custard was swept up by the sawdust wranglers, and fresh sawdust was strewn across the ring (a good word, 'strewn', it means 'strewn' (I can't really put it any better than that)), the clowns made their honking, merry way out of the tent.

'You coming, Fizz?' Mr Stump said, getting up. 'Let's go tell your mum how silly she was.'

'Um, actually, Dad,' Fizz said, staying in his seat. He felt a bit embarrassed. Of course he wanted to congratulate his mum, but he also wanted to . . .

'What is it, son?'

'I thought I'd hang around here if that's okay. There's an act I want to see.'

'An act? Isn't it all dogs and dancing this afternoon? I didn't think you liked dancing.'

'No, it's not them. It's before them. You see, I sort of made a friend the other day and she's —'

'*She?*' his dad said, in the way that dads do when a boy mentions a girl for the first time.

'Dad!' moaned Fizz.

'Okay, okay,' his dad said, holding his hands up in a *whoa-your-horses* gesture. 'What does she do, this girl you *just happened* to make friends with?'

'Flerrajin,' said Fizz, muttering it in just the same way Alice had the first time she'd mentioned the act.

'Flerrajin?' his dad asked.

He pulled the timetable out of the inside pocket of his Strongman's leopard-skin and gave it a look. Then he turned it the right way up and gave it another look.

'Botanic Act,' he read. '*Botanic?*'

'It means flowers,' Fizz said.

'I knew that,' his dad replied, mock-snappily. 'I may have muscles, Fizz, but I've also got a . . . Oh, what's it called? You know, that grey thing? Spongy? You keep it in your head. Um . . .'

'Brain?' Fizz offered.

'That's it. I do have a brain as well as all this brawn, Fizz. I know what Botanic means.' He thought for a moment, setting that brain of his to work. 'It's been years since I've seen a Flower Arranging act. It's an old one, a rare one that. Not a lot of people have the skill. What's her name, son? Maybe she's from one of the old-time families, handing down classic acts, forgotten acts, keeping them alive.'

'Alice,' Fizz said. 'Alice Crudge.'

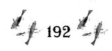

'Crudge!' his dad shouted. 'She's a Crudge!?'

Fizz was startled with his father's reaction. It was unexpectedly excited. (When Strongmen get excited it's important to keep things like glasses and biscuits and carrots (for example) out of their hands, because they tend to break things with over-enthusiastic involuntary squeezing. (Maybe we can have a bit of audience participation with the book at this point. (Not every book has audience participation, and I think there's probably a reason for that.) Please take a moment to imagine to yourself, or to discuss with a friend, some other examples of things an excited Strongman or Strongwoman should be kept away from. I bet you come up with some really funny ideas. If you think your

ideas are even better and funnier than mine then please don't hesitate to write them down on a postcard and send them in to one of those competitions they have on *Blue Peter* or other popular television shows. Do not send them to me.))

'What is it, Dad?' Fizz asked, looking around to make sure there weren't any glasses or biscuits or carrots to hand. (There weren't.)

'Avuncular Crudge was the greatest Strongman I ever saw,' his dad said, calming down a little. (There was a tiny trickle of steam coming from one ear, but other than that . . .) 'He retired twenty years ago, I was only a lad when I saw him, but he was amazing. I had his poster on my bedroom wall. He could lift the back end of an elephant. I'll show you his autograph when you come

home. It's the only one I ever collected, that and your mother's. And you know his . . . ?'

'Granddaughter, I guess,' Fizz said. He remembered Alice saying something about her grandad being a Strongman. He'd believed her, of course, but hadn't imagined he'd been such a famous Strongman, not when she was trudging around with a cicrus like *Neil Coward's*. Something must have gone wrong for the Crudges since Grandpa Avuncular's day.

'Oh, I'd love to meet her, Fizz. I bet she knows some stories. Why don't you invite her round for tea or something?'

'I'll see what I can do,' Fizz said. He wasn't sure he really wanted to share his new friend with his parents quite yet. 'Say "Big butter-fingers" to Mum for me, will you?'

'Oh, okay,' said Mr Stump, remembering he was meant to be going off to congratulate the clowns. 'See you later, Fizz.'

The lights dimmed around the Big Top. A spotlight lit up a spot in the ring. And there was Alice.

Dressed in sequins, and with a botanical headdress made of bright green plastic leaves, it took Fizz a moment to recognise her. She looked so funny.

From behind her back she whipped an untidy bunch of flowers. (I don't know much about flowers and neither did Fizz, so the descriptions in this bit of the book aren't going to be brilliant, I'm afraid. Do you remember the trouble I had describing fish in the last book? Well, it's that all

over again.) With a flutter of her hands she started whizzing the untidy flowers about.

This flower went there, that one moved round there. This one was turned to face forward, that one was shifted at a subtle angle to the left. This one was dead-headed, that one was thrown away. It was as if someone had given her a floral Rubik's cube and she was rushing to solve it in the prettiest, most elegant manner (not just one colour on each side, but patterns of complementary and contrasting colours).

When her hands had settled down, even Fizz could tell that the arrangement was *better* than it had been before. It looked neater, tidier, you could even say prettier. To anyone with the slightest artistic sense, the

new arrangement was, in fact, a significant improvement.

But, Fizz asked himself, *is this* really *a circus act?*

She put the fresh arrangement down on a little table that had appeared by her side and she turned to look the other way. There was a pause. The audience were silent in anticipation (also in not-being-there).

Then, from out of the darkness, flowers began to fly at her one at a time. She caught them and plunged them into a vase that was stood atop a second table. As each different flower arrived in her hand, she added it to the growing display, almost, it seemed, without thinking. But there was evident skill on display, because with each new bloom she added, the flower arrangement grew more impressive, more beautiful, more magnificent.

Her sequins glittered as she turned and twisted, as she caught and arranged. They sparkled. They twinkled. Her flowery head-dress moved sinuously with each movement, like a gaily coloured feathered snake down her back. (Fizz had read a book about how the Aztecs had worshipped a feathered snake called Quetzalcoatl. He had promised himself that if he ever got a pet that was the name he'd give it. It's a good name. (It's also a tricky name to spell, especially if you're typing quite quickly like I am, which explains why Fizz will *never* get a pet while I'm the one writing his stories.))

Fizz, though not entirely won over by the flowers, had to admit there was something entrancing about this show. Almost hypnotic. He'd have to ask Dr Surprise about it. Could you hypnotise someone with sequins?

And then, just as Alice held the completed vaseful of flowers above her head (it was brimful and tight-packed and as colourful as a vaseful of flowers can be (and neat as well)) something happened.

Something dreadful.

Something embarrassing.

Something shocking.

From somewhere, somewhere out in the darkness, a currant bun bounced off Alice Crudge's head and rolled to a stop on the ground.

Fortunately she wasn't hurt, partly because of the Strongman blood that flowed in her veins, the blood that gave her the strength to

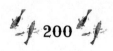

lift a full-grown sea lion without breaking a sweat, and partly because currant buns don't hurt (unless they're very stale indeed, which this one wasn't).

The currant bun was not, in and of itself, the dreadful thing I mentioned above. The currant bun was merely the prelude to possibly the most impressive, audacious bit of circus sabotage that occurred the whole of that week. The bun was the lit fuse to what was about to happen and there was nothing anyone could do but stand back and watch.

Sea lions love fish. They can sniff them out from up to one and a half miles away, if the wind's blowing in the right direction. They'll flollop, as we well know, and gobble any loose fish they can find, never mind what's in the way.

Bears can smell honey from almost as far, maybe a mile and a third. They'll track down a hidden store of honeycomb and gorge themselves until they fall asleep with sticky patches all round their mouths and bees buzzing in their dreams.

A clown can sense custard (possibly they smell it, although scientists have suggested some other new, previously unknown sense might be at work here, since clown's noses aren't actually *real* noses) from as far away as (maybe) six or seven yards. Unless restrained they will run towards it, trip over and make a mess.

None of these animals are attracted by currant buns. There is only one animal in the whole of nature whose thoughts turn to currant buns in the autumn and it just happened that one of these impressive, majestic beasts travelled with the *Franklin, Franklin, Franklin & Daughter* circus. (It didn't do an act itself, it just liked some of the guys on the crew and followed the circus around. But no one, not even Mrs Franklin herself, could think of a way to turn this circus guest away.)

And so it was that Alice Crudge, Bold and Talented Flower Arranger Extraordinaire, found herself being lifted up and set aside, placed gently, if rudely, out of the way of the currant bun, by a long curling, grey and bristled snake that twisted down out of the darkness behind her.

At least that's what Fizz's first thought was, but then he corrected himself. He wasn't stupid, that was no snake. It was an . . .

And the person operating the spotlight obviously thought the same thing and turned

the knob which widened the arc of the light. No longer was there a tight bright circle focused on Alice and her flower-covered tables: there was now a wide pool of light that held within its eye not only Alice, her tables, her flowers and a currant bun on the floor, but also the front end of an elephant: trunk, tusks, high grey forehead, big flappy ears – an elephant.

Alice was furious.

The elephant ignored her stamping. It picked up, delicately with the tip of its trunk, the currant bun and popped it back into the darkness of its half-hidden mouth.

Its little black eye was looking around for more buns.

The thing about an elephant is (and you don't need to be an expert to know this) one

currant bun does not make a whole meal. It doesn't even make a snack. To an elephant a currant bun is about the size of a small mint, maybe half a humbug. When an elephant has finished one they almost always want another one.

Fizz realised the elephant was looking around, this way and that, for a second bun. That little black eye was twirling, the nostril end of the trunk was waving around, sniffing up great gouts of Big Top air, searching for where the next mini-snack might be.

And then it lifted a whole flower arrangement out of its vase and stuffed it into its mouth. The flowers aren't currant buns, it seemed to be saying with its small sad eyes, but they are vegetables of some sort or another, and we elephants are vegetarians: we

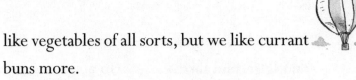

like vegetables of all sorts, but we like currant buns more.

Alice wouldn't stand for this any longer. She pulled her headdress off and stomped over, fearlessly, in front of the elephant.

'Look,' she shouted. 'Those are my flowers and you're ruining the show. If you don't leave right now I'll have to make you leave. I'm not kidding!'

She was waving her fist at the elephant to emphasise her point and pointing back towards the Big Top entrance where the elephant had come from. She wasn't sure the elephant understood English, but she reckoned the thing would surely understand such basic sign language.

The elephant showed no sign of understanding or moving.

It picked her up in its trunk and set her aside a second time.

Nobody set aside Alice Crudge twice.

She was fuming now.

Fizz was worried, partly for Alice, and partly for the elephant. He knew that a Strongman's powers were only increased by this sort of thing. His dad very rarely got angry, but once when the telly had broken just before the end of a whodunit he'd been enthralled in for the last hour and a half, he had gone outside, picked up the caravan and said several rude words. (He had then put it down, come back in, apologised to Fizzlebert and his mum, sat at the little table and wrote a letter to the television manufacturer complaining about their shoddy production values and another one to the BBC (the British

Broadcasting Corporation, not the British Board of Circuses) asking whohaddunit it in the whodunit.)

Fizz wanted to run down into the ring and rescue her, to push the elephant aside and sweep her to safety. But he was afraid she'd be even more upset by him running into the middle of it, as if she couldn't handle a little hiccough like this on her own, as if she needed a boy to ride to the rescue. From the little time he'd spent with her Fizz had the strong impression that she was happier being a *rescuer* rather than a *rescue-ee*.

Nevertheless, Fizz slowly made his way down through the rows of empty chairs to the ringside, ready to offer help if she asked for it.

But by the time he got there it was all over.

Alice Crudge, set aside for the second time in five minutes, walked up to the hungry elephant, still sniffing for buns, and put her hands around the cool rough grey trunk. When she was happy with her grip she looked the elephant square in the face, braced her legs, leant back and began to pull.

'Come on,' she said.

Her muscles rippled. Sequins flew off her outfit, landing twinkling, twirling in the dust.

She tugged and the elephant tugged back.

It snurfed, a big breath that sent dust clouds up in the air. It rumbled an unhappy noise that shook deep inside Fizz's stomach, rattling his bones.

This wasn't a happy elephant, but then again, this wasn't a happy girl.

She heaved and pulled and turned around so she was facing away from the mighty beast. She had the trunk over her shoulder, like a fisherman might have the rope of his boat as he hauled it ashore, and she began walking.

The elephant stood its ground.

Alice dug in her feet, leant forward and heaved.

Fizz was sure he saw the elephant's trunk begin to stretch, like elastic. He half-believed he was going to see it twang back and send Alice flying, but he'd read enough books about elephants to know that that wouldn't happen (he'd read one book). An elephant's trunk is not made of elastic. It's made of nose.

Where the nose goes, the rest follows, as the old saying I also just made up has it.

And so, with heaving breaths and bulging biceps, Alice kept on. Foot after foot she plodded through the sawdust of the ring. And the elephant, trying to pull itself away from this tight grip, began to slide.

Alice Crudge was pulling an elephant!

'Come on!' she shouted. 'Get out of my show!'

The elephant, presumably with a sore nose, gave in, gave up and began walking after her. It was better than being dragged through the sawdust. It was more dignified, and elephants are big on dignity (they're big on most things, but dignity is near the top: an embarrassed elephant is something to behold, they blush all over).

Alice had won!

Alice had tug-o-warred an elephant and won.

Fizz was excited for her. He thought this was one of the most brilliant things he'd ever seen. He just knew *he'd* never be able to put on a display like that. He was strong, sure, but this was way out of his league. She was

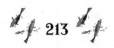

so impressive. Just wait until his dad heard about it.

He looked over at the judging table, where Mr Gomez and Wystan's amnesiac mum and dad were sat. He expected to see wonder on their faces, but instead Mr Gomez had a big frown.

Fizz edged closer and overheard him loudly saying, 'But it's not *botany*! If she'd said it was an animal show, maybe . . . But this isn't Flower Arranging as I know it. Zero points.'

And in the ring something else was happening.

Alice had let go of the elephant and it was busy wandering away from her, out into the sunshine, where there might be more chance of finding another currant bun. She slapped its bum as it went by.

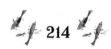

With a bead of sweat on her brow and her sequins scattered she looked like a real Strongman. But then a man came running into the ring, passing the retreating elephant with barely a glance. Fizz recognised him as her father, who he'd met once before, in a similar circumstance.

'Young lady,' her dad was shouting. 'What have you done!? Your costume!? Your flowers!?'

'Dad,' she said, trying to explain.

'You've ruined everything,' he said, not getting any quieter, even though he was closer to her now. 'Everything your mother and I have worked for. The years of training, for this! What were you thinking? An elephant, darling? An elephant! How did you think *that* was going to work? And look at your costume. It's ruined. It took me hours to sew those sequins. What am I . . .'

And so on.

Fizz felt so sorry for Alice, as she followed her dad out of the tent.

'But it wasn't me,' she was saying. 'There was a currant bun . . .'

And Fizz reckoned he knew just where that currant bun had come from. It had been dark when it had been thrown, so he couldn't be sure, but who else would have thrown it? Who else had a personal grudge against poor little harmless Alice? Who had she punched on Fizz's behalf? Whose ego had she bruised? It was so obvious that it would've been dreadfully disappointing had this book been a whodunit, which, fortunately, it isn't. (Cedric definitely did it.)

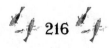

Wystan was right, Fizz suddenly thought. Cedric Greene didn't just need beating in the competition, but he also needed a long slow slurp of his own medicine. He needed bringing down a peg or two. He needed a good dose of revenge, and Fizz was just the boy to give it to him.

With that thought he made his way out of the Big Top and began looking for his friends, leaving the three sets of dancing dogs to dance without him.

CHAPTER NINE

In which a bearded boy dresses
up and in which revenge is
visited upon the deserving

Fizz looked for Wystan at dinner that evening, but he wasn't around. This was odd, because the bearded boy liked food (he liked it so much he usually kept some in his beard for later. There was a time when he wouldn't eat with other people because of this habit (when the prim and proper Lady Barboozul was in charge), but

nowadays people had just to take him as he was.).

Fizz scraped his leftovers into the bin, added his plate to Cook's washing-up pile and went off in search of his acrobatic accomplice.

The first place he went to search was at Miss Tremble's caravan. It wasn't a very long search. As Fizz walked towards the caravan he saw a beard and a boy walking (together) towards it from the opposite direction.

When they got closer Wystan said, 'Hello,' in his usual grumpy voice.

'Hi, Wystan. I missed you at dinner,' said Fizz. He then paused for a moment and looked his friend up and down. 'Wystan,' he said. 'Why are you dressed like a baby?'

(What you couldn't tell from my telling you that Wystan was walking towards his caravan from the opposite direction was that he was, as Fizz so rightly observed, dressed as a baby. He had a nappy on, done up with a big safety pin. He had a rattle in one hand, a couple of little bows in his beard and a damp dummy in the other hand (damp because he had pulled it from his mouth just before saying, 'Hello,' to Fizz). The reason I didn't tell you that three paragraphs earlier was that I didn't want to spoil the surprise when Fizz said, 'Wystan. Why are you dressed like a baby?' It's one of my favourite lines in the book and I wanted it to retain its full impact.)

'You made me think,' Wystan said, rattling his rattle in an annoying manner. 'All those things you said, ways of getting memories

back and all that. I thought that the last time they saw me, I mean the last time they saw me when they still knew who I was, before they flew away and got lost . . . Well, I was just a baby back then. I thought maybe if I jumped out at them like this, gave them a shock, it might jog their memories. So that's where I've just been, back to the farmhouse. As they were going in for their dinner, I jumped out rattling this thing.' (He rattled the rattle.) 'And do you know what?'

'What?'

'It didn't work.'

'What happened?'

'They said, "Hello," and went indoors. They didn't even seem very surprised.'

Fizz felt for his friend. He could imagine a small bit of what it must be like to

be ignored, rejected, forgotten like that. It must be dreadful. He couldn't help but think of his own parents, back in their caravan watching telly. As embarrassing and annoying as they sometimes were, at least they were there.

He had come to see Wystan with an idea which, although it might not make him feel

much better, might take his mind off his problems for a while. This was the time to say it.

'Wystan,' Fizz began. 'This afternoon Cedric struck again.' He described the scene with the currant bun and the elephantine interruption. 'You know you said you wanted to get your own back? Well, count me in.'

'What about Alice?'

'She's in enough trouble with her dad,' Fizz said. 'He was dead upset about her act going wrong. I don't want to get her in any more trouble, so let's leave her out of this.'

'Okay,' mumbled Wystan between sucks of his dummy. 'Fine.'

'Now, you said you had a plan?'

'I've got a *sort of* idea, Fizz,' Wystan said. 'But you're the real brains round here so see what you think.'

'Fire away.'

So Wystan told Fizz his idea of a plan and Fizz listened and came up with some extra ideas and they put them altogether and came up with what they agreed had to be the absolutely best plan for revenge on a boy called Cedric anyone had ever come up with for at least a fortnight. (Maybe three weeks, even.)

The next morning they would put it into action and the bullying leather jacket-clad sabotaging show-off would get his comeuppance. Ha ha! (That's how they actually said it, with a 'Ha ha!' at the end, because that's what all good evil master-plans of revenge

have at the end of them. Trust me, I know a thing or two about revenge (by which I mean I saw a play once with some in).)

And no, before you ask, obviously I'm not going to tell you their plan.

The following morning the boys met outside the Big Big Top.

'Are you ready?' Fizz asked. 'Did you get the *stuff*?'

'Yeah,' said Wystan, patting his beard.

'Excellent,' Fizz replied, rubbing his hands together.

'Hi, guys,' Alice called, running over. 'What's happening?'

'Happening?' Fizz sputtered.

'Yeah, you're looking all suspicious. Like you're spies or something. You're skulking.'

'Revenge,' said Wystan, picking a slice of stale gherkin from his beard and eating it.

'Cedric?' she said.

Wystan nodded.

'Brilliant,' she said. 'What's the plan?'

Reluctantly Fizz outlined what was going to happen and Alice pointed out where she could come in useful and the boys agreed and the three of them made their way into the gloom of the Big Big Top.

That morning Mr Gomez was watching all the 'Animal (Wild (Dangerous))' acts, of which, between the six circuses there were only three.

First up was Ranaman Smith (no relation) from *La Spectacular De La Spectacular De La Rodriguez' Silent Circus Of Dreams*. He took

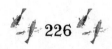

to the ring as his circus band played mighty, magnificent, martial music. It was blaring and jarring and daring and had there been an audience there they would have been expecting tremendous things.

Smith pulled off his smart animal trainer's jacket to reveal a bare chest, threw his top hat aside to reveal a bald head, and pulled a small box from his pocket to reveal a small box.

As the band hushed themselves and a drum roll rolled across the ring, he, slowly, masterfully, opened the box. Inside were little dark wriggling shapes Fizz could barely see.

Ranaman Smith then, in front of literally twenty-six eager(ish) spectators, seemingly without a thought for his own safety, proceeded to wrestle as many as almost three leeches.

Fizz hadn't seen an act like it.

'What are they?' Wystan asked, squinting.

'Leeches,' Fizz said, checking his timetable where he'd made a note of the acts they had to see before Cedric (he wanted to be ready).

'They're very small.'

'Yep,' Fizz said. 'They're leeches.'

'Are they actually dangerous?' Alice asked.

'They suck blood,' Fizz said, remembering what he'd read a few weeks before in *Robots in the Amazon II: Rusty's Canoe of Danger*, a very bad but enjoyable novel. 'And some of them carry parasites. That could be dangerous.'

'Hmm,' Alice said.

As Fizz watched the act he thought of Apology Cheesemutter. People might call the man mad for putting mouse ears on dogs, but they couldn't deny that he did it for the right reason. Mice *are* much too small to be seen in the circus ring, and leeches were even smaller.

As Ranaman Smith jumped to his feet, sawdust scattering, holding aloft the last of the leeches, the tiny foe finally vanquished by the mighty wrestler, an applau (which is what you get when there's not enough clapping to add up to 'some applause') echoed across the Big Big Top and Fizz looked down at his programme.

'It's Captain Fox-Dingle next,' he said.

The Captain had a much better idea of what made an interesting act than Smith had. He

swept into the spotlit arena riding on the back of the low green form of Kate, the crocodile, like a surfer. When they reached the centre of the ring he jumped off, lifted his hat, bowed low and waited.

After a moment Kate lunged forward, snatched his hat between the tip of her huge jaws, and snapped it backwards so it somersaulted through the air and landed on her head, just above her eyes.

Fox-Dingle and Kate went through a number of tricks: he got a broom and she chopped it into ever smaller pieces, until it was just sawdust on the ground; he got a lion tamer's chair and she chopped it into ever smaller pieces, until it too was just sawdust on the ground; he produced a pack of cards and the crocodile picked one (ate the

rest) and Fox-Dingle showed the audience the card she had picked (he had meant to say beforehand which card it would be, but he forgot (which was lucky because she'd messed up)).

Then, for their *pièce de résistance* (a French term meaning 'the Good Bit') the Captain knelt down beside Kate and watched as she opened her mouth wide. He looked as if he was going to do it, going to put his head in there just as Fizz had used to do with Charles, but at the last moment Fox-Dingle drew back and shook his head.

A watermelon rolled out of the darkness towards him. He lifted it up and balanced it on Kate's lower jaw. Her many sharp and wickedly pointed (and very real) teeth held it in place.

Captain Fox-Dingle stood up.

He raised his right arm in the air.

He paused.

The moment went on.

And then he clicked his fingers . . .

. . . and SNAP!

The watermelon exploded into a thousand sweet wet flying fragments as Kate slammed her mouth shut.

Wystan nudged Fizz in the ribs. 'That could've been you,' he said.

Fizz gulped.

He'd seen the Captain practising, and knew exactly what he had done (which was to watch very, very carefully for the moment that Kate would snap (there was a glimmer in her eyes a millisecond beforehand, he said) and click his fingers right then. To an audience member

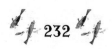

it would look like he had complete control of her, whereas in actual fact she only *sometimes* listened to him.).

As the Captain and Kate left the ring (to a smattering of genuine applause) there was a faint *beep beep beep* as the digital alarm clock in her belly struck the hour.

Finally, the moment they'd all been waiting for arrived.

The third of the animal acts was about to begin.

Into the ring marched Cedric Greene with Major Winch-Hardly (*A Ring & A Prayer's* lion tamer, an upright woman in a uniform like Captain Fox-Dingle's (but green) with a nose like an eagle's beak, sharp narrow eyes and a quality showbiz smile) and their lion, Coconut.

Cedric was wearing his leather jacket and looked around the Big Top as he walked in, lifting his hands and blowing kisses to the imaginary audience. *What an idiot*, Fizz thought, ungenerously.

'What an idiot,' Alice said, equally ungenerously, but out loud.

Wystan muttered something into his beard that no one could quite make out. It probably wasn't a compliment.

Major Winch-Hardly put the lion through a number of tricks – sitting up, rolling over, balancing on one leg, juggling meat, the usual stuff.

'When . . . ?' asked Wystan.

'Not yet,' said Fizz. 'It's gotta be at the right moment.'

'Should we get ready though?' Alice asked.

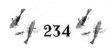

'I suppose,' said Fizz.

He knew that the 'putting the boy's head in the lion's mouth' would be the finale of the act, it had to be, and he wanted their revenge to happen then. That way Cedric would know it was meant for him in particular and not just the lion act in general. (Fizz felt bad messing up the act for the Major and her lion. After all, it wasn't them who'd thrown fish and currant buns at the other acts, they didn't really deserve having their act sabotaged. Cedric, though, deserved everything that was coming to him.)

Wystan pulled a couple of things out of his beard. There was a floppy bit of rubber, there was a little metal canister and there was a small cardboard box.

He shook the contents of the cardboard box into the floppy bit of rubber, which the more observant of you will have already noticed was a deflated balloon, then he attached the neck of the balloon to a nozzle on the little canister. With a twist of a valve and a hiss of gas the balloon rapidly inflated. Wystan tied it off and handed it to Fizz.

They had sat well away from anyone else (not that there were many other people around) and in the darkness of the Big Top they were sure this had all gone unnoticed.

In the ring Major Winch-Hardly had had Coconut (a silly, undignified name for a lion, I agree) balance on a ball, walk a low wire (which is like a high wire, but lower (lions don't mind heights but don't like ladders)) and now she had her sit up straight and open her mouth. (As

you know female lions are the most dangerous ones in the wild, they're the ones who do most of the hunting and all that, but in show business it's the male lions who get all the attention. And that's because (a) they're not as intelligent as the female lions and so don't mind living in cages so much, and (b) they're the ones with the fancy hairdo. Coconut, who was an old girl, wore a fluffy mane-wig, because that was what people expected.)

Cedric, who up to this point had been assisting the Major with the tricks (holding her hat when needed, handing her the lion tamer's chair and so on), stepped forward. This was it, this was his big moment.

Fizz took the balloon from Wystan and bopped it out towards the centre of the ring. Being filled with helium, it floated up and up.

'Can you do it?' he asked Alice.

'Oh yes,' she said. 'Easy.'

She took a cornflake Wystan pulled from his beard and perched it on the top of the last knuckle of her middle finger. Holding the tip of that finger down with her thumb, she lifted her hand up to her face, shut one eye and lined the finger up with the balloon.

'Not yet,' Fizz said, a hand in the air. 'Not yet.'

He wanted the balloon to be in the perfect position before she fired.

Not yet, not yet.

'Now!'

Alice Crudge flicked the cornflake with all the strength of her finger (which, considering it had played no small part in her

238

pulling an elephant yesterday, was nothing to be sneezed at).

The cornflake whizzed through the air. It was so small and moved so fast they couldn't see it, but they did see the balloon burst, high up in the topmost tent flaps of the Big Big Top.

(Nobody heard the pop. The balloon was far away, and the audience was small and focused on the lion-related event in the ring.)

The powder with which Wystan had filled the balloon shimmered in the air as it fluttered slowly, mistily downwards towards the circus ring.

'Is this going to work?' Wystan mumbled, as much to himself as to anyone else.

'It was your idea,' Fizz said. 'Of course it's going to work.'

'Yeah,' Wystan said, deadpan. 'I'm also the one who thought dressing as a giant baby would work, but . . .'

'That's different.'

'A giant baby?' Alice said, turning to look at the bearded boy.

'The ring! Look in the ring,' Wystan said, pointing.

The dust cloud from their balloon had reached the ring. It was impossible to tell it apart from all the rest of the ordinary dust that was in the air, not unless you'd followed it all the way down.

Cedric was leaning over, his head almost inside Coconut's wide open mouth. Major Winch-Hardly was stood to one side, her hat jaunty, her whip handle twinkling, ready to intervene when the time came.

And then something happened.

Something wonderful.

Something funny.

Something embarrassing.

(All Fizz and his friends had wanted to do, it should be noted, was embarrass Cedric the way he'd embarrassed them. Of course they didn't want to *hurt* him, didn't want to put him in *danger*. They just wanted to give him a taste of his own medicine and see how he liked it.

Of course, it's at this point I should give you a little lecture about revenge. Being the author, I have to take some responsibility here. Revenge is one of these things that makes sense in a novel, but probably isn't so good in real life. If we all lived by the code, *An eye for an eye and a tooth for a tooth*, meaning *Do back to them what they done to us*, then we'd be fumbling around knocking soup bowls over all the time, and where would that get us?

That's the end of the lecture. Now, back to the story.)

As Cedric put his head in the lion's mouth the lion, Coconut, sneezed.

When a lion sneezes it's not a pretty sight (not as bad an elephant, perhaps, but still . . .).

Their noses are much bigger than yours or mine and they're more full of . . . well, to put it delicately in case there are readers of a sensitive disposition out there, more full of 'the sort of things noses are full of'.

Anyone who's read any of these books before will remember that Fizz's lion, Charles, had a set of rubber false teeth he wore for the act, and luckily old Coconut was the same, so when she sneezed Cedric wasn't bitten in two, but he was trapped with his head inside a sneezing lion's mouth and with her nasal expulsions (a polite way of saying, *excuse me*, 'snot') all down his back.

As the cloud of pepper had drifted down from the balloon it had settled, bit by bit, on the delicate surfaces of everyone in the ring's noses.

Inside Coconut's mouth, not only was Cedric trapped, but he too was sneezing. Have you ever had anyone sneeze when their head was inside your mouth? Especially when you feel like sneezing again yourself, when your eyes are beginning to stream and when the boy in your mouth is flailing his arms and legs about? (No? I am surprised.)

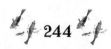

Coconut wasn't happy. She sneezed again, splurging more green gunk and goo further down Cedric's back. Cedric sneezed again, banging his head on her tongue, pulling at her lips with his hands and doing a strange sort of involuntary dance with his legs.

Major Winch-Hardly, who was sneezing herself (the pepper cloud having reached her at the same time as the others), tried her hardest, between blowing her nose on her handkerchief to say, 'Nut! Drop!' and to tap the lion on the shoulder.

The old girl spun round, surprised at the tap, pulled Cedric off the ground, and swung him (accidentally) into the lion tamer's head, knocking the sneezing Major to the floor. Coconut's mane-wig came loose and flew across the ring, leaving the poor lioness naked and embarrassed.

A naked and embarrassed lioness (even one trained for circus tricks) isn't what we generally call a Good Thing.

'Oh no,' Fizz said when he saw that Winch-Hardly wasn't climbing to her feet. 'I think she's been knocked out.'

Wystan said, 'Uh-oh.'

Alice said, 'We've got to help. Fizz, what do we do?'

Fizzlebert was the only one who knew *anything* about lions. He was the one who'd have to go down there. He knew it. He had caused the trouble and he'd have to set it right. Oh, why had he been so set on revenge? So what if the boy had teased him and got Fish in trouble?

But this was no time for thinking, he thought, this was a time for doing.

He stopped thinking and did.

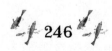

'Wystan,' he said. 'Go get Fox-Dingle. He must be around somewhere, he's only just left.'

'Aye aye,' said Wystan, running off between the chairs.

'Alice, you're with me. Keep your distance and keep safe, but come with me.'

He clambered over the rows of chairs between them and the ring as quickly as he could. Alice was vaulting them beside him.

In the ring the lion was going mad. It had finally spat Cedric out in a big pool of spittle and snot and was roaring with peppered misery, flashing its gums at anyone who went near, rearing up, sneezing and rattling its claws threateningly.

Cedric was rolling around, a pair of rubber false teeth wrapped round his neck, moaning and crying.

Mr Gomez and the two Xs were sneezing and cowering behind their judges' table as the lion paced nearby.

Fizz grabbed Winch-Hardly's lion tamer's chair and approached Coconut from behind.

'Here kitty, kitty, kitty,' he said, holding the chair before him. 'Come to Fizzlebert. Leave the nice people alone.'

The lion ignored him, roared at the judges and swiped their table with a huge clawed paw. It left four long deep scratches in the wood.

'Kitty, kitty, kitty,' he shouted, to absolutely no reaction.

So, with his heart pounding in his ears, Fizz edged nearer, leant down and stamped on the lion's tail. (Don't try this at home.)

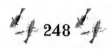

He had to get its attention, get it away from the judges.

'That's right,' he said as Coconut spun, roaring, and slashed at him with shining claws. 'Hello! Over here, puss!'

Fizz held the lion tamer's chair out in front of him, in between him and the lion, and backed up a few steps.

He needed to get the lion to follow him.

Back a few more steps.

Coconut, growled, lunged, roared and took a few steps in his direction.

That was it.

'Alice,' he shouted over his shoulder, not sure where she was. 'Get them out of here.' He nodded towards the judges.

(Alice ran round the ringside while the lion was distracted and heaved each of the judges

up into the seats, out of the ring and out of the lion's reach. While Fizz kept Coconut distracted she ran and tossed Winch-Hardly over her shoulder and pulled Cedric to his feet. She cleared the ring of bystanders. She did her job.)

'Here kitty, kitty, kitty,' Fizz repeated, backing up further. He wasn't sure what else to do. His training as a lion tamer hadn't extended this far. Captain Fox-Dingle had done this bit. All Fizz had ever done was stick his head in the lion's mouth and hold his breath. And besides, Charles had been a lovely old thing, not like Coconut, who was embarrassed, angry and (did I mention?) *sneezing*.

Fizz felt an itch in his nose.

He had to keep the chair between him and the lion. He had to keep it raised. Every time

the lion struck out with his paw the chair had to be there to block the blow. That was simple enough, but . . .

Fizz's nose was definitely itching.

The pepper!

He'd forgotten the pepper. It was still drifting about in the air.

And now it was up his nose.

He could feel the twitching itching feeling. That itch that can't be scratched because it's inside your head. It was coming, it was coming . . .

He held the chair out in front of him.

And then he sneezed.

It's a well-known fact that when you sneeze you always shut your eyes. (Some people say if you don't your eyeballs will fly out, but I don't know if that's true, and neither do scientists because no one's ever got ethical clearance to do the experiment. Do not try *this* at home, either.)

When you shut your eyes a lion will always attack. (Not *every time* you shut your eyes, of course, only when there's a lion stalking you already. I don't want to make anyone afraid to blink.)

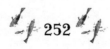

And Coconut did (attack, that is). She lunged, past the chair, which dipped as Fizz sneezed, and caught him a blow across his shoulder that tore the epaulettes off his old Ringmaster's coat and sent him, sneezing and tumbling to the ground.

Fizz lay in the sawdust and thought, *Oops*.

Even a lion with no teeth, if it's angry enough, can be a dangerous thing to lie down in front of.

He tried to get to his feet, but his head was spinning and his arm was numb. He wobbled.

He slowly climbed to his knees.

Where was this lion?

(The tent was spinning too.)

And then he heard voices.

'Fizz! Fizz!' It was Wystan's voice. Wystan, his friend.

And a sharp, 'Good girl.' That was Fox-Dingle. Oh! Wystan had found the Captain.

He was the finest lion tamer Fizz knew. He'd be able to deal with Coconut, no worries.

Wystan helped Fizz to his feet and Fizz stood there for a moment brushing himself down.

'Look at that,' Wystan said, turning Fizz to face the other way.

There was Alice. Alice Crudge, Flower Arranger Extraordinaire, holding, above her head, on its back with its claws flailing harm-lessly in the air, Coconut the lioness.

'No worries, Fizz,' she said. 'No need to thank me.'

'Thank you,' said Fizz, needlessly.

After she'd put the lion down and Captain Fox-Dingle had taken charge and walked

Coconut back to her cage, where the revived Major Winch-Hardly took over, Alice and Fizz and Wystan were stood outside the Big Big Top.

Fizz's wounds weren't wounds at all. He'd have a bruise on his shoulder, and his right-hand epaulette had gone flying to who knew where, but that was as bad as it got.

'Wow,' he said. 'That was close.'

'Yeah,' said Wystan grumblingly. 'I sort of wish we hadn't done that.'

'Done what?' said Cedric, lurching over to them.

He still had the rubber teeth round his neck and he was covered in lion slobber. His leather jacket was shredded and he was limping a little (probably for show). He wasn't really hurt either, but his ego, his dignity and his sense of humour had all taken pummellings.

'Done what?' repeated Fizz, trying to think of a good answer.

'Rescued *you*,' said Alice.

That was the good answer Fizz would have said had he had more time to think. She was smart as well as strong and all the rest of it. Fizz blushed.

'I don't know how you did it,' Cedric sneered, 'but I'll get you back. You've not heard the last of Cedric Greene.'

And with that the obnoxious boy, dripping with slime and snot, hobbled away.

'Well,' said Fizz, to the other two, 'I reckon that's over now. That's the last we'll see of him. At least we know he's not going to be picked for the big show.'

'And neither am I,' said Alice.

'Nor me,' added Wystan.

'Looks like it's gonna have to be you, then, Fizz,' Alice went on, putting a hand on his shoulder as she spoke. 'You and your dad. I can't wait to see it.'

As if mentioning him made him appear, Mr Stump came running up. 'Fizz! Fizz, there you are. I heard there was an accident. Are you guys okay?'

He swept Fizz up in his arms.

'It was nothing, Dad,' Fizz said, wriggling out of his dad's extremely embarrassing (and strong) embrace.

'They're saying you saved the day, Fizz. You rescued people –'

As if there weren't already enough people in this scene, and as if Wystan didn't already feel bad enough about not having any parents

(who knew who he was), Mr Crudge came running over too.

'Alice,' he shouted as he got near. 'I hear you've been showing yourself up again. Embarrassing the family by juggling cats or something. What have I told you about silliness? All the time we put in –'

'Dad,' said Fizz, quite rudely, but kindly, interrupting Alice's dad. 'This is Mr *Crudge*, and this is my friend Alice.'

Mr Stump's moustache perked up with delight when he heard the name. His eyes grew huge and glittered like glitter.

'Oh, Mr Crudge,' he said, grabbing the other man's hand and pumping it vigorously, 'I was *such* a fan of your father . . .'

And while Mr Stump distracted Mr Crudge with his ebullient praise and relentless

admiration, the three kids slipped away unnoticed.

'You know what,' Fizz said to Alice with a shy, sly grin. 'I've just thought up *another* plan. A good one.'

CHAPTER TEN

In which a double act is performed
and in which an ending (and
a sea lion) comes in sight

That afternoon there were four acts
being seen by Mr Gomez in the Big Big
Top.

He had a box of tissues on his table just in
case.

First up were three sets of plate spinners.

Mr Crudge was first and he spun three
plates all at the same time, but seemed

distracted, uneven, and lacked the true finesse the real top-notch plate spinners have.

Next Abigail Air came out and not only spun three plates at once, but also incorporated some juggling into the act. She smiled and shimmered and told jokes while keeping her crockery rotating at high speed, but there were some mutters about whether juggling belonged in a plate-spinning act. Nevertheless, she finished with a confident dismount (all three plates in one hand) and a generous bow to the judges' table.

Then Percy Late came out and spun his plate beautifully, elegantly, uniquely.

After the plate spinning it was time for the final act on the timetable. The Strongman.

(Mr Stump wasn't the only Strongman in the six circuses, but Arthur Tonne (of *The All-Inclusive Hypoallergenic Circus Of Small Surprises*) had come down with a nasty rash the week before and was still in recovery, and Tiny Jake (of *Franklin, Franklin, Franklin & Daughter*) had tripped on a potato and twisted his neck. (I should point out that there was nothing suspicious about either of these occurrences. Just because there has been sabotage elsewhere in the book I don't want you to be thinking there's any here. Being a Strongman is a risky job, you're putting your body under enormous strain (if you're doing it right) and sometimes things snap. Everyone understood that.)

As it stood, Mr Stump (and Fizz) were the only Strongmen competing for a place in the

Circus of Circuses show, but that still didn't mean that they'd automatically go through. It depended which acts Gomez and his fellow 'judges' thought (by which we mean, 'Gomez decided') were the best acts *overall*. It could be that Saturday's show had six clown acts, for example, or it might be it had none. No one could ever know in advance (the running order wasn't announced until Saturday morning).

I should probably have explained all that earlier on. Sorry.)

Anyway, Mr Stump and Young Mr Stump (*Stump & Son*) were the last act to be seen.

They walked out into the ring to a ripple of applause (there were more people there than usual (round about forty-six), since everyone was now at a loose end until the announcement the following morning).

Fizz was wearing his Ringmaster's coat and a top hat he'd borrowed from Dr Surprise (it was his spare spare hat). His father was carrying a safe under his arm. Fizz was carrying a cake under his.

They went through all their tricks out there in the ring. Playing catch with big rocks, juggling dumbbells, attempting to eat Madame Plume de Matant's cake. They lifted audience members in the air, two at a time (and twirled them). They balanced the safe on Mr Stump's head and Fizz stood on top of it and opened the door with a sledgehammer. Inside were gold bars (actually lead bars painted gold), which they took out and piled on top of Mr Stump's outstretched arms. His muscles bulged and wriggled until he bounced the bars into the air and Fizz

caught them one by one in a pyramid-shaped stack.

Eventually Mr Stump hauled a car into the ring on the end of a rope which he pulled with his teeth. (It was his wife's clown car, but still, a car is a car.) And, kneeling down, and with help from Fizz, he hefted it up on to his back. From there he stood up (with Fizz balanced on the car's roof) and lifted it above his head.

It was brilliant. It was spectacular. It wasn't over yet.

Fizz reached down inside the car and pulled out –

But hang on!

Something silvery came flying through the air and slapped Fizz right across the face.

Something that smelt fishy.

Another silvery something slapped down on to the roof of the car.

There was a distant honking, barking noise from somewhere outside that almost everyone who heard it over the music recognised. (I would be personally disappointed if *you* didn't recognise it after all we've been through together.)

Fizz, on top of the car, looked down and kicked aside the sprat or mackerel or whatever it was (definitely a fish of some sort). It fell to the ground beside Mr Stump's foot with a wet thud.

Mr Stump looked down.

'Fizz,' he called. 'I think you've dropped a fish.'

And then bursting through the Big Big Top's flapway came a shape that we've all seen before, doing exactly the same thing it did in Chapter Four. It was Fish and he was after the fish that had mysteriously appeared in the ring.

A charming red-headed boy stood up in the front row of the audience and jumped into the ring.

'Cedric,' he shouted. 'It's the same thing! You've done the same thing again! This is rubbish! Have you no imagination? Cedric, where are you?'

As this mysterious boy was shouting out, looking for Cedric Greene, Fish was hurtling across the ring exactly like a fish-seeking sea lion. (I was going to say 'like a fish-seeking missile', but it wasn't quite the right simile since, as far as I know, no such missile has ever been built.)

He skidded in the sawdust and slid across the ground, mouth first and mouth open, ready and eager to gobble the slick silvery sardine that lay by Mr Stump's feet. The momentum of his movement sent him straight through Mr Stump's legs, knocking them aside and sending him tumbling to his knees.

The car wobbled and the figure of Fizz on top wobbled too.

'What's going on?' he shouted down from above.

'It's okay,' Mr Stump shouted up from below. 'I've got a good grip. Don't panic. Just climb down.'

But as the car rocked the other fish slipped off the roof and thudded to the sawdust.

Fish whipped round at the salty noise and his flipper brushed Mr Stump very lightly, but in just such a place as to be momentarily ticklish.

An involuntary flinch from Mr Stump sent the car tumbling.

A worried horn hooted somewhere off in the audience.

Fizz fell from the car's roof, top hat tumbling, long reddish blonde hair flapping out in the breeze.

He landed on the judges' table flat on his back and, looking up, saw the car coming straight at him. Without thinking, in a move of lightning instinct, he held out his hands and lifted his feet just as the car thudded down on top of him, the table and the judges.

His arms buckled and the car continued its downwards plunge.

Mr Gomez fell backwards in his seat and landed safely out of harm's way with a crash on the floor. But Mr and Mrs X weren't so smart and the falling clown car, slowed but not stopped by Fizz's quick reflexes, ever so gently tapped them both on the very tops of their heads.

'Ow,' they said together.

Fizz rearranged his grip on the stalled car, flexed his arms, used his legs as levers, and

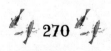

tipped it up and off him. It thudded to the ground in front of the judges' table and all the doors fell off.

'Thank you, young lady,' said Mr X, rubbing his head. 'We've met before, haven't we?'

CHAPTER ELEVEN

In which things are explained and in
which all the loose ends are tied up

Hang on a minute . . .

Mr X has had a bump on the head and
suddenly he can't tell girls from boys?

No. It's not that straightforward. If you
recall at the end of Chapter Nine Fizz said he
had *another* plan. Let me let you in on the plan.

Fizz's coat fitted Alice Crudge perfectly.
They were the same height, more or less the

same build. If she tucked her hair up into a hat then from a distance (and, remember, most of the audience is at a distance in the circus, (hence the 'mice')) then no one would be able to tell the difference. Fizz's dad, though sorry to not be doing the act with Fizz, was (on the other hand) stupidly excited to be doing the act with a real live Crudge: the super-strong granddaughter of his biggest hero, Avuncular Crudge. And Alice, for her part, was equally over the moon to be performing with her all-time hero, Mr Stump.

If it was possible, Fizz had realised, to make two people so happy so easily, simply by giving something up, then there was really no choice. It had made him surprisingly happy to do it too. It was funny, he'd spent the whole week worrying that he didn't have an act

of his own, the past few days fretting about Cedric's threats and bets, but when the time came none of that seemed important, not compared to the look on their faces and the warm glow in his heart (which is all slightly sickly to tell you, but true).

Fizz and Alice didn't explain to Mr Stump quite how mad it would make her dad to know that she'd been doing an actual real live Strongman show, but what harm could that do?

As it happens, when he found out about the act (putting his plates away back stage, he heard the commotion in the ring and came out in time to see her hat fall off and her hair fall out (of her hat, not her head)), he came storming over and was about to tell her off, when Mr Stump patted him on the back and told him how amazing Alice was. Mr Crudge tried to get a word in edgeways, but Mr Stump sat him down and went on about her brilliance, her skill, her strength until Crudge sighed deeply, shook his hands in the air and said, 'Okay! Okay, Stump, I give in.'

(It turned out, Mr Stump later told Fizz, that the famous Crudge strength had skipped a generation. Mr Crudge had no more muscle than a normal man. That lack in him was what made him overly protective of Alice. Mr Stump explained it away by saying 'psychology', which is a big word that just means, 'the mysterious human mind, who can explain it?').

Fizz was sorry though that he couldn't do anything for Wystan. It had been so easy to make Alice and his dad happy, but Wystan had missed out on everything. Even the revenge they'd undertaken had left a sour taste in their mouths. He wished he could have waved a magic wand and given Wystan his parents back, but magic wands are the sort of things you only find in books.

He had been worrying about this during the show, but once Cedric had started throwing fish he'd pushed it to the back of his mind. *That Cedric*, he thought, *I'll show him*.

And so Fizz (the real Fizz) had climbed down into the ring and shouted for Cedric. He'd looked around the seats searching for the boy.

Little Simon Pie, clown-in-training and early Cedric/Fish victim, had been the first to spot him.

'He's over there,' he'd shouted, honking his little horn and twirling his bow tie for attention. Cedric was quickly tracked down by a gang of angry clowns and dragged out on to the sawdust.

His hair was lank and lifeless, his face pale and angry, and, even though his leather jacket was shredded like a Morris dancer's tassels, he still wore it draped over his shoulders like a security blanket. He no longer looked cool, and when he chewed his fingernails he did so nervously, like everybody else.

This was the last afternoon's trial and Cedric hadn't counted on so many people being around. He hadn't thought so many people would be there to see Fizz's new act (even if Fizz wasn't actually in it). But they'd

all heard of the *original* Boy Who Put His Head in the Lion's Mouth and wanted to see what he was going to do next. (He'd been in the BBC's Newsletter *twice*. People had heard of him.) Or at least that was what Fizz secretly chose to believe.

What Cedric especially hadn't counted on was his dad being in the audience that afternoon.

'Cedric Greene,' boomed the Ringmaster. 'What have you been doing?'

'They . . . They,' Cedric stuttered, pointing at Fizz, 'they poured pep-pep-pepper on my act.'

Fizz, not a lad to whom lying came naturally, said nothing and hummed a little.

'Empty your pockets,' Cedric's father demanded.

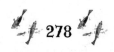

Moaningly, Cedric did as he was told.

Fish, fish, handkerchief, loose change, comb, fish.

'This boy,' Ringmaster Greene said, pointing at Fizzlebert. 'This boy and this sea lion –' he pointed at Fish '– have been used by you for *nefarious* ends. I am disappointed. Mr Gomez is disappointed. Our circus is disappointed. Disappointed, I say!'

'But,' Cedric snivelled, 'I did it for you, Dad. I did it to give us a *chance*.'

'And I gave *you* a chance, Cedric. I listened to your whinging. I bought you a lion, I hired the second-best lion tamer I could find. And what did you do? You wasted the opportunity. Winch-Hardly can do the lion act herself. She's a good chap. Doesn't complain. Shouldn't have to put up with you going round making her lion sneeze all the time. Next week it's back to candles for you.'

Aha! That was it. Fizz had *thought* Cedric did an act involving fire and he'd been right. Cedric was the assistant to Ronald Birthday, *The Master of Breath*. Ronald could blow out two hundred candles with one breath (he did other tricks with his breath too, not just blowing out candles (though that was the one people remembered)) and Cedric was the boy who lit the candles. Ha ha!

'But, Dad,' the boy whined as his father sent him away.

'Fizzlebert Stump,' Ringmaster Greene boomed before he left too. 'Apologise to the sea lion for me.'

Fish had already gobbled all the fish from Cedric's pockets. He belched a sprat-scented

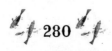

burp and wandered off in search of more food.

Fizz looked around and noticed there was a commotion round the judges' table.

He went over.

'My hands are *blistered*,' Mr X was saying.

'And mine,' said his wife. 'Look at those.' She held her hands up.

'That tractor seat is uncomfortable. And you'll need a bigger one soon, Gomez.'

'What do you mean?' the farmer asked.

'For your fat bum,' Mr X said, angrily.

'How long were we there? Stuck on your farm? How long's it been?' asked Mrs X.

'A little while,' Mr Gomez wheedled. It was obvious he didn't want to give a precise answer.

What was going on, Fizz wondered. *Had they . . . ? Hang on!*

'Wystan,' he called, 'get over here.'

But Wystan was already on his way.

'Have they . . . ?' he asked, breathlessly.

'I don't know,' said Fizz, 'but I think so.'

Gomez saw Wystan coming and shouted, 'No! No, *you* keep away!'

Mr and Mrs X both turned as one and what they saw set their moustaches curling.

'Wystan?' they shouted together. 'Is that you?'

And it was.

'Oh, you've grown so. Oh my! Our boy! How long's it been?'

Wystan told them.

Mr X turned to Mr Gomez and said, '*How long?*' as if he couldn't quite believe what

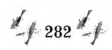

Wystan was telling him. But it was obviously true, he'd been a little bouncing bearded baby boy when they'd gone off on that final flight and now here he was practically grown up.

'It all seems such a blur,' Mrs X was saying. 'The years have all been a blur, like a dream.'

Like a blur, *maybe*. Like a dream, *perhaps*. But they remembered enough of what had happened to them to know that they'd been done wrong, that they'd lost whole *years* of their lives on the farm, that because of Mr Gomez and his laziness and his wickedness they'd missed out on watching their boy grow.

And by now other people were taking an interest in what was going on and pretty soon the story of the bearded boy and his missing parents was all round the six circuses.

'You mean they're not French?' people were saying. (Madame Plume de Matant came out of hiding when she heard that.)

'You mean they've been made to *work* the farm? With *those* vegetables?' people said.

'Parents of the bearded boy?' they asked. 'That means they're *circus folk*, practically.'

If there's one set of people you don't want to get on the wrong side of, it's circus folk.

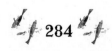

284

For a start a lot of them are slightly peculiar, many of them are rather odd, a few of them have weird powers, and all of them stick together. Never mind a bit of sabotage here and lively rivalries there, at the end of the day they were one big family. That was it. That was the bottom line. Simple as that.

Mr Gomez tried to explain how he had taken in two poor amnesiacs and cared for them, nursing them all the time slowly back to health. He explained how he gave them a little work to keep them occupied and how kind he was to involve them in all aspects of the farm and the Circus of Circuses show each year. Was that not enough to prove he was a Good Man?

The six Ringmasters looked him up and down and told him firmly: No. It wasn't.

They weren't going to get the police involved, were they?

The six Ringmasters told him, equally firmly: No. They weren't.

They were going to do things the circus way.

They were going to give him the Cold Shoulder.

There would be no Circus of Circuses show tomorrow, nor ever again at *this* farm.

They wrote a strongly worded letter to the British Board of Circuses which was published in the very next Newsletter and soon every circus in the country knew what Mr Gomez had done to two of their own. No circus would ever go within four and three-quarter miles of his farm and if ever they found he'd bought a ticket to one of their shows, he would be refused entry and given *no refund*.

(The BBC also wrote him a letter asking for his certificate and badge back. When he didn't reply they sent a crack squad of ninja-clowns who stole them while he was distracted.)

Mr and Mrs X, now answering to the names of Wilfred and Hester Humphreys, pulled their old hot air balloon, *The Golden Goose*, out of the barn where Gomez had hidden it. With the help of the men, women and elephant of the circuses the balloon was patched and inflated.

On Sunday morning they and Wystan climbed into the basket.

Fizz held one of the ropes and said, 'Is that it then? Are you really off?'

287

Wystan stroked his beard and said, with a sad smile, 'I've got 'em back, Fizz. Thanks to you and Alice, and thanks to Cedric even. I've got 'em back and I've gotta go with 'em, haven't I? We've got places to be, places to see. People to go visit and surprise with aerial music.'

And how could Fizz argue with that?

He stepped back. Alice put an arm around his shoulder. He blushed, but didn't push it away.

'He'll be back,' she said.

Fizz shrugged.

His mother, who was stood the other side of him, parped her horn solemnly and blew her nose loudly on a red handkerchief twice the size of an average-sized tablecloth (not a big one, just an average-sized one (one half the size of a big one)).

Almost the whole of the six circuses had gathered in the farmyard to watch the balloon lift off.

Through a chorus of 'farewell's and 'good luck's and 'bon voyage's there came a honking, barking, flolloping noise and the crowd parted as Fish charged his way towards the rising basket.

'Fish,' shouted Wystan. 'Goodbye!'

And Fish, instead of launching himself through the air to land in the basket beside his bearded pal (as Fizz secretly hoped he might), flicked his head and tossed a silvery treasure high into the air. It cartwheeled and turned in the late autumn sunshine and landed with a wet slap at Wystan's feet on the floor of the basket.

'Gosh, that stinks,' said Hester Humphreys as she reached down to pick it up.

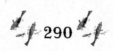

'It's a fish, Mum,' Wystan said, grabbing the sprat for himself.

'Well, it pongs,' she said, with a smile.

'I'll chuck it if you like. I mean, if you want me to.'

They were already high above the farm now. All his friends and colleagues looked tiny down there.

'Oh no, don't do that,' said Mr Humphreys, Wystan's father. 'It was a gift. You must always keep gifts.'

Wystan looked at the gift. It was cold and slippery.

His dad went on, 'You must always keep gifts, Wystan, at least until you're out of sight of the gift giver.'

'Let the wind take us far away,' his mum said. '*Then* chuck it, love.'

She gave the switch a turn and a gush of flame lit the inside of the balloon above them.

They rose higher.

'Okay, Mum,' Wystan said, waving a last farewell over the wickerwork.

On Monday morning the six circuses began packing away their tents and loading up their caravans ready to head back out on the road (in six different directions).

Fizz scuffed his feet in the dirt outside Alice's caravan, waiting to say goodbye to her before she left. There were butterflies in his stomach, which was weird because the Ringmaster had specifically asked Cook to stop serving caterpillars up in the pasta (again). (And for anyone who's thinking,

'But at the end of *Fizzlebert Stump The Boy Who Cried Fish* Cook was hypnotised into being a super-good chef why would he be serving caterpillars up?', I have only two things to say: (1) it was Dr Surprise who did the hypnotising, and (2) these were *gourmet* caterpillars.)

Alice came down the steps and said, 'Hi, Fizz.'

'Hi, Alice.'

'This is goodbye then.'

'Yeah, I suppose so.' He kicked at the dust. 'I hear you had an offer.'

'Oh yeah,' she said, grinning broadly under her twisted nose. 'Ringmaster Rodriguez has invited us to join their circus. I'm going to be their star junior Strongwoman and Dad's going to help out in the costume department. He loves sewing sequins and all that. It's going

to be brilliant being in a real circus at last. No more spelling mistakes for us. The Crudges are back!'

Fizz was happy for her, but there was still something fluttering in his stomach all the same.

'I'd hoped you might join *us*,' he said, quietly.

'Don't be silly, Fizz,' she laughed. '*Stump & Son* is Strongman act enough for any circus. I'm ever so grateful to you for letting me be a Stump for a day. But . . .'

'No worries,' Fizz said. 'And no need to say thank you.'

'Oh well,' she said. 'It's been cool. See you around sometime?'

'Yeah,' Fizz said, trying to sound as cool as she did. 'See you around sometime.'

She punched him on the arm in a friendly way and went up the steps back to her front door.

(He would cherish the bruise.)

'Oh,' she said, quickly running back down. 'Take this.' She kissed him on the cheek. 'That's for your dad.'

Before all the circuses went their separate ways Fizz had one last visit to make.

He picked his way between the caravans of *A Ring & A Prayer* until he found the one that Cedric was cleaning. He was using scraps of soft leather to polish up the windows.

'Oh, it's you,' he spat. 'Stump.'

He almost seemed to be afraid, the way he hunched as Fizz walked up.

'Hey, Cedric,' Fizz said, trying to sound friendly.

'What do you want? Come to cause more trouble?'

'No, I just wanted to say that since neither of us really did our acts, and since neither got picked for the show, I don't expect you to write that letter to the BBC Newsletter. You don't have to say I was the best Boy Who Put His Head in a Lion's Mouth. It's all right.' Fizz held his hand out to shake. 'I forgive you,' he added.

Cedric looked at the hand as his brain listened to the words.

'I wasn't going to write a letter, Stump,' he muttered. 'Even if you had won.'

'I know,' Fizz said. 'But I would've.'

And with that, hand unshaken, Fizz turned around and walked back to his own

296

circus, where his mum had a stack of warm salmon and gammon sandwiches waiting for him.

He smiled to himself. Oddly, strangely, even with his friends going off and knowing that Cedric didn't like him, he felt happy. There was a new beginning here: *Stump & Son*.

And really, who knew what tomorrow might bring?

Mr Gomez knew what tomorrow would bring. Tomorrow and every day for the next thirty-six years was spent farming his seven fields of unnamed odd-shaped vegetables and dreaming of the circus that he loved so much but which he never, ever, ever got to see again. That taught him a lesson and a half.

Now, if this book were a television show, then there'd be one final scene before the theme tune strikes up and the end credits roll.

It would have some members of the regular cast, say Fizz and his mum and dad, sat having their lunch and discussing what they'd all learnt from this week's adventures. Then after the moral had been driven home with a sledgehammer, they'd all laugh at some really lame joke with really fake laughter.

But this book isn't a television show. There are no lessons to take away and the book actually finished with the one-sentence paragraph about Mr Gomez being sad and lonely and doomed to work his farm forever because he kept some people who really needed medical attention as his own personal unpaid farmhands and then got found out.

So maybe there is a moral after all: don't get found out.

But then again it might be something else. I don't know, I just write this stuff, you're the one who's read it all. Maybe you know what it was all about?

Anyway, thank you and well done.

That's the end.

You can shut the book now.

LOOK OUT FOR FIZZLEBERT'S PREVIOUS ADVENTURES